Twenty minutes later, I made it to the other side of the island. I stopped and checked my cell phone. The blue dot was beginning to fade, indicating the thirty-minute tracker was dissolving, but from what I could tell, Eduardo was to my right.

I rode into a deserted parking lot of the state park. Behind me stretched a half mile of beach highway leading back into town. In front of me spanned the dark ocean lit only by the half moon. To the left stood a small concrete visitor's station.

With the DNA glasses still on, I scanned the area. A red trail led from the parking lot, where the car must have dropped him and drove off, and onto the beach.

Leaving the bike, I followed the red trail across the beach and down the length of a long pier. The red trail stopped at the end of the pier, where a boat had probably picked him up.

There was no telling how far out he'd gone.

I unsnapped my pocket and pulled out the cell phone. I activated the audio recording/eavesdropping software Chapling had coded in.

Here went nothing.

OTHER BOOKS YOU MAY ENJOY

the specialists
the winning element

shannon greenland

speak

An Imprint of Penguin Group (USA) Inc.

SPEAK
Published by the Penguin Group
345 Hudson Street, New York, New York 10014, U.S.A.
Penguin Group (Canada), 90 Eglinton Avenue East, Suite 700,
Toronto, Ontario, Canada M4P 2Y3 (a division of Pearson Penguin Canada Inc.)
Penguin Books Ltd, 80 Strand, London WC2R 0RL, England
Penguin Ireland, 25 St Stephen's Green, Dublin 2, Ireland
(a division of Penguin Books Ltd)
Penguin Group (Australia), 250 Camberwell Road, Camberwell, Victoria 3124, Australia
(a division of Pearson Australia Group Pty Ltd)
Penguin Books India Pvt Ltd, 11 Community Centre,
Panchsheel Park, New Delhi - 110 017, India
Penguin Group (NZ), 67 Apollo Drive, Rosedale, North Shore 0632, New Zealand
(a division of Pearson New Zealand Ltd)
Penguin Books (South Africa) (Pty) Ltd, 24 Sturdee Avenue,
Rosebank, Johannesburg 2196, South Africa

Registered Offices: Penguin Books Ltd, 80 Strand, London WC2R 0RL, England

Published by Speak, an imprint of Penguin Group (USA) Inc., 2008

10 9 8 7 6 5 4 3 2 1

Copyright © Shannon Greenland, 2008
All rights reserved
Library of Congress Cataloging-in-Publication Data
Greenland, Shannon.
The specialists : the winning element / by Shannon Greenland.
p. cm.
Summary: GiGi, the teenaged computer genius, gets to lead her first mission, trying to catch a
notorious chemical smuggler who years ago was responsible for the deaths of her mother and
father.
 [1. Spies—Fiction. 2. Orphans—Fiction. 3. Genius—Fiction.] I. Title. II. Title: Winning
element.
PZ7.G8458
[Fic]—dc22   2007020206

Speak ISBN 978-0-14-241052-3 (pbk.)

Printed in the United States of America

ACKNOWLEDGMENTS

A shout out goes to Sandra Giles and the West Nassau Warriors! Thanks for letting me hang with you for the day and learn what exactly a scorpion is. Ouch!

the specialists

the winning element

∷[proloque]

SISISSY. SISISSY. dI-did yooouuu hear wh-what I aaassskkked yo-you?

Sissy pried open her heavy eyelids and focused on the fuzzy image of Ms. Gabrier. The teacher's lips were moving, but Sissy couldn't make out her words.

Ms. Gabrier stopped talking and stood still.

From across the classroom Sissy squinted, bringing her teacher into focus. She was looking right at Sissy.

Ms. Gabrier's lips started moving again. Her words filtered into Sissy's ears, slowly swirling through her head, echoing off her skull in distorted vowels and syllables.

Sissy dragged her dry tongue around her mouth, trying to moisten it, and smacked her lips. She needed a soda.

Faintly, she heard some giggles, and in her blurry peripheral she saw other students laughing at her.

So what? She could care less. Let them and their perfect little selves laugh.

"Sisissy?"

Dragging her head from the top of her desk, Sissy slouched, sliding her butt down in her chair. She propped her boots on the desk in front of her and let her eyelids fall back down. Sleep. Beautiful, much needed sleep.

"*Sisissy?*"

"What," she grumbled. Couldn't they see she wanted to sleep?

"Priscilla," Ms. Gabrier snapped.

Sissy's eyes shot open. "What?" she snapped back. *Nobody* called her Priscilla.

Her teacher's eyes narrowed. "Do you realize you're failing this class?"

Sissy shrugged. Of course she realized she was failing. She never turned in any homework or studied for tests. Her mom didn't care. No one cared. Sissy's life wasn't going anywhere, anyway. And why did teachers always ask stupid questions that they knew you knew the answer to?

"All right." Ms. Gabrier jabbed the off button on the overhead projector. "You know what?" She pointed her pen at Sissy. "I've had enough of you. I don't care if you *do* have the highest test scores in the school. I don't want you in here. If you don't care, I don't care. Look around you. Look!" her teacher shouted.

Sissy jumped, took her feet off of the desk, and sat up straight. She'd never heard her teacher raise her voice.

Ms. Gabrier's jaw tightened. "I said *look*."

Suddenly very awake, Sissy dragged her gaze over the thirty or so other students in Advanced Chemistry. Mostly preps and nerds. Everyone was college bound. Some with scholarships, others with Daddy's and Mommy's money. All of them were staring back at her with mixed expressions. Haughty, disgusted, amused, pitying, scared.

Scared of what? Scared of her?

Ms. Gabrier tapped her nail to the podium. "Do you see any of them sleeping through this class?"

Sissy swallowed.

"Do you?"

She barely shook her head.

"That's right. Because they know what an honor, what a *privilege*, it is to be in here." Ms. Gabrier placed her pen on the podium. "There are exactly seventy-one students on the waiting list to be in this junior class. Do you know how many students are on the waiting list to be in this high school?"

Sissy shook her head.

"One thousand eight hundred and twenty-three."

Silence.

She'd had no idea that many kids were on the waiting list.

"You were placed in the Jacksonville Academic Magnet School because of your brilliance. This school made the top ten list in the nation. Do you know how incredible that is for a public school?" Ms. Gabrier closed the teacher's edition lying on her podium. "What a waste. I'm tired of trying. This is what it's like day in and day out with you . . . when you're here."

Ms. Gabrier pressed her fingertips to her temple. "I'm done. You're out of here." She closed her eyes. "Go fry your brain on drugs in someone else's classroom."

The blond girl beside Sissy snickered.

She turned and snarled back at her. Why did everyone assume Sissy did drugs? She was just tired. Exhausted. Working the night shift at the Laundromat to make enough money so she wouldn't have to rely on her mom would do that to you.

Her teacher punched the projector back on. "Jami, please escort Sissy to the office. And Sissy, take all your stuff. You're not coming back."

▓ ▓ ▓

Thirty minutes later, Sissy climbed in her friend Courtney's open window. She snatched a piece of gum from the pack on the dresser and caught sight of her reflection in the dingy mirror.

She looked wasted. No wonder everybody always thought she was.

Heavy black eyeliner smeared her puffy bottom lids. Day-old black lipstick crusted her dry lips. Her dyed black hair stuck out in short, gelled clumps. And the bruise from last week's fight with her mom still colored her chin.

Ms. Gabrier was the only teacher who had asked about the bruise. Sissy had told her she got in a fight with a friend. It was a better excuse than "I ran into a wall." Who actually believed that anyway?

The other teachers had seen the bruise. How could they not? But none had asked. If you asked, then you had to follow up. Paperwork, reporting to authorities, blah, blah, blah. Who had time for all that junk? None of the teachers cared. Or at least none cared when it came to Sissy. Now if it had been cute little Kirstie or peppy, athletic Lisa . . .

Whatever. Everyone expected this from Sissy. Bruises, drugs, zeros.

Outside, a train bumped by, rattling the apartment walls. Sissy plopped down across the unmade bed and popped the gum in her mouth.

She should've botched the stupid state test that put her in the academic magnet. That way she'd still be in her old school with Courtney. At least there Sissy hadn't stuck out like a freak.

But she hadn't been able to resist the temptation to see, just to *see,* how she would do on the test.

Sissy knew she was smart, even though she'd made D's and F's her whole life. No one else had thought she was smart. In fact, she'd been recommended to attend a "special" school once.

She snorted. "Puh-lease." A "special" school?

Showed how much they knew.

Sissy blew everyone away when she aced the state test. Thinking back on it brought a smirk to her face.

She toasted the air with her middle finger. *Here's to everyone who ever thought I was a loser.*

The bedroom door creaked open. Pam, Courtney's mom, peeked in. "Oh, hey, Sissy. Thought you were Courtney."

Sissy didn't bother reminding Pam that it was eleven in the morning and Courtney was in school. Pam wouldn't care one way or the other anyway.

Dressed in a long T-shirt and boxers, Pam shuffled across the worn carpet to the dresser. She opened the top drawer, pulled out a pair of socks, and slipped them on. "Aren't you supposed to be in school?"

Sissy shrugged. "Got kicked out." Story of her life.

Tucking her wet brown hair behind her ear, Pam leaned back against the dresser. "Me and Courtney are moving back in with her daddy."

Sissy got really still, knowing what came next.

Pam took a deep breath and then blew it out slow. "You can't come with us. I know your momma booted you out again, and I'm sorry. But me and Courtney's daddy, we got enough to work on without you tagging along."

Why me? What did I ever do to anybody to deserve this reject of a life? Sissy pushed the irritating voice in her head aside. It did no good to give in to the depression. "When do you want me out?"

"End of the day." Pam glanced over to the black garbage bag that held Sissy's clothes. "I got an old suitcase if you want."

"It's all right," Sissy mumbled, rolling onto her side to face the window. She'd lived with Courtney and Pam on and off over the years. A week here, a month there. They let Sissy come and go as she needed, whenever her mom brought another guy home, whenever they fought, whenever her mom drank, whenever she got violent . . .

Behind her, Pam left the room.

Outside, another train approached, sounding its horn.

Sissy chomped down on her gum. *What am I supposed to do now?*

THAT EVENING SISSY SQUATTED UNDER the bleachers of Jacksonville Magnet, surveying the school's gym. The night janitor locked up, crossed the parking lot to her truck, and drove off.

Sissy waited in the grass, smacking at Florida's enormous mosquitoes, watching the school for any more activity. Humid air hung heavy around her, making her baggy clothes stick to her skin. She spit her gum into a wrapper, put a new piece in her mouth, and continued to wait.

Thirty minutes passed, and the coast stayed clear. Sissy picked up her bag of clothes and jogged across the football field to the gym. She rounded the side to the boy's locker room, popped open the vent leading into the showers, and crawled through.

The smell of bleach overpowered her senses, and Sissy murmured a quick thank-you to the janitor gods. Two nights ago when she'd come, the janitor had been sick and the place had been a disgusting mess.

She tiptoed through the dark locker room, out the door, and down the hall to the windowless boiler room. She didn't know why it was called the boiler room when all it held was old classroom junk. Tons of it. Broken copy machines; old wood desks; books, books, and more books; rolling chalkboards; bulletin-board paper; storage bins; old gym mats.

And chemistry supplies.

Sissy walked in and flicked on the desk lamp.

She'd come across the place by accident. At the end of last school year she'd seen the janitor unloading desks off a cart. Sissy had stopped to help. After all, the janitor *was* old.

But the janitor had left without securing the door, so Sissy was able to rig it not to lock—easy to do with a gum wrapper—and went back that night.

And again the next night.

And the next.

All summer long she'd gone, slowly making it into her space and escaping life. Many nights when she didn't work, she slept over, using the girl's locker room to shower.

She'd be here tonight. No way she was crawling back to her mom.

Sissy wound her way through the dusty desks to the big wood chemistry cabinet. Hidden beneath it, she pulled out her notebook.

Her spirit lightened as it did every time she lost herself in her experiments, her solutions, her chemicals. Years ago she'd found a kid's chemistry set in the garbage and pulled it out. She'd cleaned it up and followed the instruction manual carefully as she'd composed her first basic experiments. And her life had never been the same since.

She smiled at the memory. Being here in this makeshift lab was the only time she was in a good mood. The only time things felt right. *She* felt right. Her life didn't suck.

Flipping through the notebook, she scanned the handwritten pages, searching for the metcium formula . . . ah, there it was. Something about it wasn't right, and she'd puzzled over it for a week straight. Then it hit her last night as she was folding clothes at the Laundromat.

Beside the chemistry cabinet stood a stack of poster boards propped up against the wall. Hidden behind them was her box of supplies.

Sissy moved the poster boards aside and slid out her box. Any spare money she had she spent on chemistry supplies. Some legal, some not. A good majority of her powders and liquids were her own derivatives of marine life. Easy enough to obtain when you lived in Jacksonville, Florida.

She opened the box and carefully pulled out flasks of ciumdroxide, coloride, and trosesineo—all highly flammable liquids. From the cabinet she got two rubber mats, a burner, two beakers, and some stirring rods.

Sissy carried all the supplies over to the desk. She unrolled a rubber mat, spread it across the desktop, and then placed a smaller one on the floor for her to stand on. Both would absorb any electricity created from her work.

She put on her goggles and rubber gloves and got down to business. . . .

As she poured the trosesineo into the beaker that held the coloride, her experiment consumed her. Her concentration mixing the two liquids held her total focus. Any other time she would've noticed the flame getting too high. She would've paid attention to the ciumdroxide she'd already put to heat bubbling too close to the edge.

In her peripheral vision through her goggles, she caught sight of the ciumdroxide a split second before it boiled and foamed over the edge.

She jerked her head up, accidentally bumping the flask of trosesineo. It toppled over, flowed straight into the boiled-over ciumdroxide, and both liquids immediately caught on fire. Sissy's heart lurched as she reached for a fire extinguisher at the same time pink smoke preceded a bright flash. Then an explosion sent her flying backward.

▦ ▦ ▦

AN HOUR LATER, SISSY SAT handcuffed beside some cop's desk. How stupid could she have been? She'd *never* lost track of her experiments. If it weren't for the gym mats she'd landed on, the explosion could've caused some broken bones.

With a sigh, she glanced over to the left where a coffeemaker sat on a small table. Some old guy had just made a fresh pot, and it smelled heavenly. In front of her sprawled the station's open workroom with desks placed here and there. Each desk had a phone and a computer. No walls separated them. Only three other cops were present this late in the evening.

The cop beside her hung up the phone. "Your mom doesn't want you."

Sissy could've told the cop that and saved him a phone call.

His chair squeaked as he leaned back. His red hair and baby face made him look about the same age as Sissy. Sixteen. He probably had just got out of cop school.

He folded his hands over his skinny stomach. "What about your dad?"

"I don't have one."

"What do you mean you don't have one? Everyone has a dad."

Where'd this guy grow up? "Well, I don't."

The cop frowned. "What do you mean?"

Sissy ground her teeth together and wished for a piece of gum. Why'd they take her gum anyway? It wasn't like she could break out of jail with it. "I mean, I don't know. I don't know his name. I don't know where he lives. I don't know anything. Zilcho. My mom doesn't even know." How much more did Sissy have to spell it out?

Sissy's father could be any number of men. Of course she'd always fantasized that he was some famous chemist, that she'd inherited her talent from him.

Whatever. Not like her mom would ever be with some famous chemist.

The cop's chair squeaked as he brought it back down. "What were you doing with those chemicals?"

Sissy shrugged. "Nothing. Just playing around." Little did he know, little did *anyone* know, the discoveries she'd made.

The cop shook his finger at her. "If you were making a bomb, you better come clean right now, young lady."

She nearly snorted at his sudden authoritative tone.

And a bomb? Puh-lease. She had better things to do with her time than make bombs. "When do I get my notebook back?"

His desk phone rang, and he picked it up. "Officer Roman." A few seconds passed as he listened to whoever spoke on the other end. "All right." He hung up the phone and rolled his chair back. "Let's go."

The cop escorted Sissy through the workroom and out into the empty lobby. He uncuffed her and nodded to the chairs. "Sit. Someone will be out."

"When do I get my notebook back?"

"Sit." He left and closed the door in her face.

Way to ignore my one and only question, idiot. Sissy stomped across the tile floor and sat in the metal chair farthest away. *Someone will be out.* What did that mean?

She looked across the lobby to where the front desk clerk sat. "Did someone make my bail?"

"Yes," he answered without glancing up.

Who? Who would make her bail?

Suddenly, the same door Sissy had come through opened. A chubby red-haired woman stepped out.

Ms. Gabrier?

▦ ▦ ▦

A FEW MINUTES LATER, Sissy climbed into her teacher's car. "Why'd you make my bail?"

Ms. Gabrier cranked the engine. "You're welcome."

Sissy rolled her eyes. "Thanks. Do you have my notebook?"

Ms. Gabrier pulled from the police station's parking lot. "Let's wait until we get to my house." She turned on a jazz station, and with that, they rode in silence.

Sissy stared out her window, idly watching the buildings and houses they passed, everything dimly lit by streetlights. Since it was already after midnight, there was little to no activity.

Why did her teacher bail her out? And why were they headed to her house? It didn't make any sense. Ms. Gabrier didn't even like Sissy.

Fifteen minutes later, they pulled into a neighborhood with small one-story houses, each with a tidy yard. A cookie-cutter place with nothing unique about the brick homes.

Ms. Gabrier parked in her driveway and led the way up a mulch path to the front door. She unlocked it, stepped inside, and flipped on an interior light.

She pointed to the right into the living room. "Have a seat. I'll make coffee."

She strode down a hallway into a kitchen that lay straight ahead, and Sissy turned into the living room. A blue leather sectional sofa framed the back and side walls in an ∟ shape. A circular wood coffee table sat in front of it. A bookcase ran the length of the other wall, with a stereo in the center and CDs lining both sides. There was no TV. And the whole place smelled . . . clean.

It was just the sort of cozy living room she'd always fantasized about. She had the weird urge to ask Ms. Gabrier if she could stay. Forever.

Sissy crossed the soft carpet to the bookshelves and began browsing. Some fiction, but mostly science manuals and chemistry journals lined the shelves.

"It's instant. But it'll do," Ms. Gabrier said, coming up behind Sissy and handing her a mug. "Have a seat."

Sissy followed her over to the couch. They settled on opposite sides of the ∟.

"I have your notebook. The police released it to me." Ms. Gabrier scooted back on the sofa, making herself comfortable. "It's in some sort of cryptic writing. Will you tell me about it?"

Only Sissy could decipher her personalized shorthand. "Can I have it back?"

"Yes, of course. I'd like you to tell me about it first, though."

Sissy hesitated, sipping her coffee slowly, deciding how much to say. "Experiments. I like tinkering with chemicals."

"You're doing more than tinkering. Tell me about coloride and trosesineo."

Sissy narrowed her eyes. "How do you know about coloride and trosesineo?" She'd personally created those chemicals.

Ms. Gabrier's lips curved. "I saw the terms in your notebook."

Sissy studied her teacher's mischievous smile. "Who are you?"

Slowly, Ms Gabrier rotated the mug in her hands, studying the dark liquid. A few seconds passed, and then she glanced over to the doorway, making Sissy turn to see.

A tall, dark man stood silently in the dimly lit entryway. His glacier eyes seemed to glow green in the shadows. He stepped into the room, holding Sissy's notebook. "Hello, Priscilla. My name is Thomas Liba. Ms. Gabrier and I work for the IPNC,

Information Protection National Concern, which is a special-operations division of the government."

Sissy jerked her eyes over to her teacher.

Ms. Gabrier put her mug on the coffee table as Thomas Liba came into the room. He sat down on her side of the couch's L.

"I've worked for the IPNC for thirty years," Ms. Gabrier said. "I've done a variety of jobs for them, including training." She nodded toward Mr. Liba. "In fact, Thomas was one of my trainees. Ten years ago, the IPNC placed me undercover as a teacher in the Jacksonville Academic Magnet School so I could monitor gifted kids like yourself."

Gifted kids like myself?

"The government," Mr. Liba picked up, "has had their eyes on you since last year. Since you aced the Florida state science test."

"You came out of nowhere with that one," Ms. Gabrier put in. "I did some research and discovered you'd taken plenty of state tests over the years. You didn't even try, though. Anybody could tell that if they'd taken a few minutes to actually review them."

"So what does this have to do with me?" Sissy asked.

"In the IPNC," Mr. Liba continued, "we have a group called the Specialists. They're made up of young adults your age and a little older. They're all system kids. No family. Or in your case, no family who wants to keep you close. No ties. Nobody wants them. Each Specialist is gifted in one particular area. Clearly, for you that would be chemistry. As a Specialist you are given a new identity and trained to one day go undercover."

Sissy didn't respond. She couldn't. Her shock left her mute. She sat on the sofa staring back at both Mr. Liba and Ms. Gabrier.

What is going on?

Shifting, Ms. Gabrier crossed her ankles. "Mr. Liba is here for you, Sissy. He wants you for the Specialists."

I STARED AT the picture on the conference room table as TL's words replayed in my head. *That's a picture of you and David. You lived here and knew each other when you were children.*

There stood four-year-old me with six-year-old David beside me, our arms wrapped around each other as we grinned for the camera. We were both dressed in shorts and T-shirts.

We looked happy. Truly happy.

I recognized a sequoia tree that towered behind us. It stood along the back fence close to where we were a week ago with Wirenut and Cat diffusing the hematosis detector.

David moved closer to me and leaned in. I slid the picture between us so we could both get a better look.

I was the same back then as I am now. Tall, lanky, blond. David looked different. His boyhood chubbiness had transformed into athletic hotness, and his light brown hair had darkened to almost black.

I glanced over at him. "Did you know about this?"

David shook his head.

We'd had numerous trust issues when we first met. In fact,

he'd outright lied to me. But it had all been worked out, and there'd been no dishonesty since then. Still, sometimes I found myself questioning things.

Like right now.

Obviously, when TL recruited me for the Specialists, he'd known I'd once lived here at the San Belden Ranch for Boys and Girls. And obviously, he hadn't told me; otherwise, I wouldn't be so shocked right now.

However, I'd learned over the months that TL always had a good reason for his actions. His job required a keen sense of timing, knowing when to do certain things, when to say other things. He was highly trained. Everyone knew they could trust and rely on him.

He would die for any one of us Specialists.

But still . . . why hadn't he told me? Why hadn't he told David?

"David's right," TL commented as if reading my rambling thoughts.

He did that a lot. Sometimes I wondered if he didn't have a touch of Mystic, the Specialists' clairvoyant, in him.

"David was raised here. He's always known that. This is the first he's heard that you lived here, too." TL folded his hands on top of the table. "The ranch used to be a safe house for the children of our nation's top agents. Now, of course, the Specialists train and live here."

I knew the ranch used to be a safe house. David had told me that months ago when I first moved in. I paused and slowly brought my eyes up to TL's. "So . . . are you saying my parents were government agents?"

"Yes."

I stared at him, dumbfounded, unable to comprehend fully what he just acknowledged. My parents used to be agents? It didn't make any sense. My mom had been a kindergarten teacher and my dad an insurance salesman. I had very few memories of them, but I definitely remembered visiting my mom's kindergarten classroom. I'd ridden a seesaw with a little Asian boy and practiced tying shoes on a big stuffed blue boot.

How could I have such vivid memories if they weren't true? "Did my parents live here with me?"

TL shook his head. "No. They visited you here. You have to understand, GiGi, it wasn't safe for you to be with them. They traveled constantly, sometimes together, sometimes separately."

"B-but I remember visiting my mom in her classroom. I remember going on a picnic. I remember . . ." Wait, did I *really* remember all that stuff, or had someone told me that had happened to me?

"Your memories are true." TL nodded toward the picture. "That was taken the day your parents picked you up from the ranch after they resigned from the agency. They wanted a normal life for you, a real family, which was why they moved you to Iowa. They loved you very much."

I closed my eyes as memories of my parents flooded my brain. My beautiful mother laughing. My father smiling. My parents kissing. My dad swinging me around. My mom brushing my hair.

My lips curved with the tender memory of my dad teaching me to ride a bike. My mom had been there, too, clapping and cheering me on. They *had* loved me. Very much. Sometimes it was easy to forget that simple, wonderful fact.

Suddenly, I recalled something Mike Share, David's dad, had said to me months ago. *You look just like your mother.* I'd thought he'd seen my file. Now I knew differently.

I opened my eyes. "Mr. Share knew my parents."

TL smiled and nodded. "Mike Share and your father were best friends. Like brothers."

David and I exchanged a small grin. How neat to know our parents had been best friends.

Under the table, David put his hand on my knee, and my stomach swirled. One week ago we'd been making out in the pantry, and his warm touch now gave me a quick flashback of the encounter.

He squeezed my knee. "How come GiGi didn't come here to the ranch when her parents died?"

TL sat back in his chair. "Legally, that wasn't possible. Her parents had resigned. If they'd still been IPNC employees, GiGi would've come here. As it was, she became a ward of the state of Iowa."

And I bounced around between orphanages and foster homes for the next ten years of my life.

I wanted to ask why TL kept all this from me, but I knew the answer. It wasn't the right time to tell you, he'd say.

He propped his elbows on the chair's arms. "Your parents died in a plane crash."

I nodded and looked down, a wave of sadness passing over me at the memory of the crash.

TL linked his fingers across his stomach and took a breath. "But that crash wasn't an accident."

I got very still and slowly looked at him. "Wh-what do you mean?"

He leveled serious eyes on me. "Your parents were murdered."

What?! My whole body went numb. My mind blanked. The faint sound of the air-conditioning muted to a faraway hum. I couldn't move, talk, blink. I felt paralyzed. No thoughts formed in my brain.

Only the word *murdered* echoed through my mind.

Faintly, I registered the spike in my body temperature and then the immediate chill.

TL's cell phone buzzed, and I blinked.

He checked the display. "I'm sorry. This is the head of the IPNC. I have to take this."

I felt myself nod, slowly, unconsciously.

Murdered.

David took my hand. "Come on."

I blindly followed him out of the conference room, shuffling behind him, letting him lead the way.

Murdered.

We walked around the underground, high-tech workroom and came to a stop at the elevator. David punched in his personal code and then placed his hand on the fingerprint identification panel. The elevator slid open and he led me inside.

Murdered.

I swallowed and shook my head, trying to clear the fog.

The elevator door slid closed.

David took my left hand and rubbed it between both of his. "You're freezing." He took my right hand and did the same.

As he continued rubbing my hands, I slowly regained my equilibrium. "Murdered?" I finally spoke.

He pulled me to him. "I'm so sorry. I had no idea."

I wrapped my arms around his waist and held on tight. Burying my face in his neck, I breathed deeply his wonderful, comforting scent.

We stayed in that position for what seemed like forever as David stroked his hand over my back. I replayed TL's words over and over and over again. I tried to connect with how I felt about this new information, but I couldn't quite register it all yet.

My parents had been dead a long time. I'd already dealt with that loss. But murdered? I needed to know more. How? Why?

I needed my computer.

Kissing my head, David pulled away. He punched his code on the elevator panel, and it began its ascent.

Linking fingers with me, he stared at my face, his gaze casually roaming over my features.

Usually, I got nervous when he did this, but right now, all I could think of was, "What do you see when you look at me that closely?" I hadn't meant actually to voice the question out loud.

But I had, and now it hung in the air between us.

The elevator stopped four floors up at the ranch level. Neither of us moved to punch in our code that would open the door.

With his brows drawn slightly together, he continued staring at me. And the more he stared, the more I wished I could take the question back.

He was probably trying to come up with a nice way of saying he saw the biggest, most uncoordinated geek in the world when he looked at me.

"Never mind," I mumbled, reaching for the control panel.

David sighed. "Well, I was going to ask you to go to dinner. But if I know you, you're anxious to get on your computer and research your parents."

One hour ago I would've leapt at the offer. *Our* first date. *My* first date ever. But there was no way I'd have fun. I'd be preoccupied the whole night with my parents. "Let me figure all this out. And then yes, *yes,* I want to go to dinner with you."

Leaning in, he kissed me softly on the lips. "All right, I'll hold you to it." He punched in his code and stepped off the elevator into the hallway of the ranch house, leaving his cologne lingering behind. Before the door closed, he turned and said, "If you want to talk after your research, I'll be in my room."

"Thanks," I said.

He turned again and walked away, and I stood there a minute, not even realizing that I came upstairs for no reason. Shaking my head to clear my brain, I pressed my code and the elevator descended back to Subfloor Four. Quickly, I made my way around the workroom with a wave to Adam, David's roommate, who sat at one of the black desks typing on a computer.

I walked back into the conference room, expecting to see TL and wanting to talk to him to find out more, but found Jonathan, our PT instructor, instead.

"Hi."

He glanced up, and his bald head picked up the gleam of the overhead lights. "Hey back to you," he rasped. Jonathan had a perpetual smoker's voice even though he didn't smoke.

"Seen TL?"

Jonathan readjusted his eye patch. "He's been called to Washington. He'll be back late tomorrow." He opened a folder on the table and pulled out a picture. "He said to give you this."

The picture of David and me. I took it from Jonathan. "Thanks."

I left the conference room and walked back around the workroom and down the hallway to the computer lab. I punched in my personal code and stepped inside the warm, coffee-scented room.

Chapling, my mentor, sat hunched over his station with an oversize coffee mug beside the mouse. His red-haired head bobbed as his stubby fingers raced over the keys. He didn't acknowledge me, and I didn't expect him to. Like me, he was lost in his own world pretty much most of the time.

I rolled out my chair and took a seat. I propped up the picture of David and me on the keyboard and got down to work researching my parents' plane crash.

FOR TWO SOLID DAYS, I hid out in the computer lab, investigating my parents' deaths, comparing all the newspaper articles to the TV and radio manuscripts. All the reporters said the same thing:

Our plane went down over Lake Michigan because of air in the fuel line. Out of one hundred and twenty passengers on board, only thirty-one survived. All bodies had surfaced but my parents.

We'd been on our way to Canada for a family vacation.

Some vacation.

Not one reporter mentioned anything about its not being an accident. No one thought it was strange my parents were the only bodies that did not surface.

So I moved on to investigative documents from local and state offices. Take out all the technical jargon and their reports mirrored the media's. The crash was an accident.

I went to the national level next, the IPNC, and came up against a firewall. I could've hacked through it within seconds, but chose to follow proper procedure instead—permission and a password from TL.

I knocked on TL's office door.

"Enter."

Turning the knob, I stepped inside. From behind his desk, TL glanced up and then went back to typing on his computer.

"Sir, I'd like you to give me access to the IPNC files regarding my parents' death."

He stopped typing, sat back in his chair, and brought his gaze up to meet mine.

Pulling my shoulders back, I straightened my posture. Not only did it make me feel confident, it showed my seriousness.

"When was the last time you ate?" he responded instead of addressing my request.

I thought for a second. "David brought me a sandwich at one o'clock this afternoon."

TL glanced at his watch. "It's twenty-two hundred hours right now. You haven't eaten in nine. Looking at your bloodshot eyes and the dark circles beneath them, I'd say you haven't slept much either. And I won't mention the fact that you've skipped out on every single meal, chore, training session, and your university studies."

I just looked at him. I didn't need a lecture right now.

"What exactly are you looking for?" he asked.

Although I hadn't told him what I'd been researching over the past couple days, I knew he knew.

TL knew everything.

"Answers. Discrepancies. New knowledge. Old knowledge. An understanding of what exactly happened." I had been six when that plane crashed. Until this week I'd never bothered reading the reports.

The social workers, cops, and psychologists had explained to me what had happened. I'd simply accepted it, never questioned it. Frankly, I hadn't wanted any reminders of that day.

TL pointed to the metal chair in front of his desk. "Sit."

He hadn't agreed to my request about the file access, but I closed his door and took a seat anyway. I'd take what I could get. "How do you know my parents were murdered?"

"The IPNC found your dad's body."

I sat very still, absorbing what he said. "What do you mean you 'found my dad's body'? All the reports say neither one of my parents surfaced."

"They didn't. The IPNC took your dad." He paused. "But we couldn't find your mom."

I sighed, exhausted, confused, and rubbed my dry eyes. "Will you please just explain to me what's going on? I'm too tired to figure it out."

After a long pause, he shifted in his seat. "For almost a decade, your parents followed a chemical smuggling ring. The people involved would import illegal substances into the States and resell them to overseas terrorists for manufacturing bombs."

In the time I'd been with the Specialists, I'd learned how horrible people could be, and how some would do anything for the right price. I experienced a quick flash of pride that I was a member of an organization that fought those people, the bad guys.

"The leader of this chemical ring," TL continued, "was, and still is, Eduardo Villanueva. Your father infiltrated the ring and became a member of Eduardo's team. He lived and worked with Eduardo for two years, secretly feeding information back to your mother. Eduardo wasn't just involved in the bomb business. His money filtered into all kinds of other things: drugs, guns, prostitution, gambling, murder."

I leaned forward. "So what happened?"

"Someone on the inside—we're not sure who and how—discovered your father's true identity. They found out about your mother, too."

My stomach clenched.

"Eduardo put a price tag on both their heads. Immediately following, your father and mother resigned from the IPNC and ran. They picked you up, got new identities, and moved to a small town in Iowa. They lived there for two years without a single problem."

My heart picked up pace.

"Then the IPNC intercepted a message that Eduardo knew where your parents were. We notified them immediately, and they hopped on a plane to Canada. There was a contact there waiting for the three of you with yet another set of new identities."

"I thought we were going on vacation," I mumbled.

TL scooted forward in his chair. "Eduardo rigged that plane to go down. He had divers ready. He wanted to make sure your parents died."

TL's expression softened. "The IPNC responded to the crash before local and state authorities. When we pulled your dad's body from the water, he had been shot once in the head."

I flinched, not expecting those words.

"We couldn't find your mother. We don't know if Eduardo took her body, or if it floated away with the current. But the IPNC couldn't take the chance that the authorities would discover your dad's body and the bullet hole. Then the media would've known he'd been murdered, and that would've started a domino effect the IPNC couldn't risk. So he was cremated, and, officially, your parents died in a plane crash, their bodies were never found, and they left one surviving daughter, Kelly."

Kelly. It seemed like forever since I'd heard my real name. "And Eduardo Villanueva?"

"Still being pursued by the IPNC. Every time they think they have him, he outsmarts them. He manages to slip through their fingers every time."

I sat for a good solid minute, digesting everything. "No one ever found my mom's body? So . . . she might still be alive?"

"GiGi," TL sighed. "Eduardo wanted her dead. She's dead. You need to accept that."

But if no one ever found her body . . . bull crap, I didn't need to accept anything. "Why didn't you tell me all this two days ago when you first showed me that picture?"

"I wanted to see what you'd do with the information you had. Yet another one of the many tests you will go through in your training." He paused. "Plus, knowing your personality, I knew you'd do your own research and try to find out the answers yourself."

Sometimes I didn't understand TL's reasoning. Why put me through all this? For two days I'd been down in my lab, barely eating and sleeping. All for what took him ten minutes to tell me. I closed my eyes, irritated, aggravated, and raw with the truth about my parents. My dad had been *murdered*. My mom might, *might*, still be alive.

I opened my eyes, purposefully showing him all the frustration weighing me down. "Would you have told me this two days ago if I'd asked?"

"No."

My frustration morphed into anger, and I snapped. "I don't understand you. I know you have a reason behind everything you do. And I'm sure in this instance it was something about me maturing or gaining independence or whatever. But these are my parents, and you had no right to keep that information from me."

Without giving him a chance to respond, I shot to my feet, pumped with adrenaline. "You said Eduardo Villanueva is still out there, still at large. Well, I want to go after him." I jabbed my finger in TL's direction. "And since I can't do it alone, you're going to have to help me."

2

TL MAINTAINED A dead-pan expression as I stood defiantly in front of him, staring unblinking into his icy eyes.

Silence stretched between us.

Long seconds ticked by, and my heartbeat pulsed in my neck, my veins, my temple. In the quiet room I heard only its thumping and my raspy, quick breaths.

I didn't resist the anger and sadness fueling me. I allowed it in. It felt *good*.

"I want to go after Eduardo Villanueva," I repeated. "And I want you to help me."

"I realize you're upset, but make no mistake, I give the commands around here. Not you."

His intimidating comment made my jaw tighten.

"I suggest," he continued in a measured tone, "that you leave my office to cool down and collect your thoughts before you say something you're going to regret."

"How do you expect me to sit back and ignore the fact my parents' murderer is still out there. What if it were Nalani?" I blurted out. "What if someone murdered your wife? You wouldn't stand by and calmly accept it. You'd go after them."

Every muscle in TL's face hardened. Slowly, he got to his feet. No one else but David knew TL and Nalani, our pre-op agent, were married. And until this second, TL hadn't known that I knew.

Not giving him a chance to answer, I railroaded on. "You have no hold on me. Remember, I'm the only Specialist who didn't do anything illegal on my own. You tricked me into coming here."

Somewhere in the back of my mind, I knew I was taking things too far. But I couldn't seem to stop myself. "I can walk out right now, and you can't stop me."

"So walk out then."

Suddenly, my boiling anger faded to a concentrated focus. He'd once given me an ultimatum; now it was my turn. I knew exactly what I wanted to do, without a doubt in my mind. "You have until tomorrow morning. If you're not prepared to help me find my parents' murderer, then I'm leaving."

I quickly turned and opened his door.

"Don't drop a threat," he said, his voice steady and stern, "unless you're ready to go through with it."

I turned around and looked him in the eye. "Oh, I'm ready. More ready than I've ever been in my life." And I was. I'd never been more sure of anything.

I walked out, clicked his door closed, and, with measured steps, made my way down the long hallway to my bedroom. The usual scene greeted me when I walked in.

Mystic sat cross-legged on the floor studying some sort of Tarot cards.

On her bed, Bruiser and Parrot faced each other, engaged in a rip-roaring game of thumb wrestling.

Chomping her gum, Beaker lay stretched out on the carpet, scribbling in her chemistry notebook. I wondered, not for the first time, what mad-scientist formulas she had in there.

Cat, the newest addition to our team, and Wirenut reclined across Cat's bed, sharing a set of earphones and a bag of cashews.

I experienced a quick pang of loss. Come tomorrow morning, I might never see any of them again.

I'd put it all—my whole new life—on the line.

Bruiser glanced up and grinned. "Yo! Where you been? I've barely seen you in the past two days."

Giving her a small smile I really didn't feel, I shuffled over to my bed and sat down. My tennis shoe bumped my suitcase underneath. The same dinged-up blue suitcase that had carted my belongings around the last ten years of my life.

I'd been so excited finally to unpack it, so thrilled to settle permanently into a place I could call home.

In a few hours I might be repacking the same suitcase I swore I'd never use again.

My gaze fell on the lollipop bouquet David had given me when I returned from my mission with Wirenut. With a sigh, I chose a coffee-flavored one and slipped it in my mouth.

Wirenut took his earphone out. "What's going on? You don't look right."

With that question, everyone stopped what they were doing and focused on me.

I took a second to meet each of their curious gazes.

Calm, peaceful Mystic—the clairvoyant. With his thick neck, huge body, and short blond hair, he always made me think of a football player, not an in-touch-with-the-universe kind of guy.

Red-haired, freckled Bruiser. One hundred pounds of hyperactivity. Always sporting an innocent dimpled grin and tight, customized T-shirt. Today her shirt read, HEY! YOU GOT A PROBLEM? No one would ever guess she was one of the world's best fighters.

Shy Parrot, with his dark, Native American features and sweet heart. For a guy so quiet, it amazed me he spoke sixteen languages.

Our electronics specialist, Wirenut. His trim goatee and bicep tattoo made him look like bad news. His silly humor said he was anything but.

Beside him lay his girlfriend, the beautiful, Mediterranean Katarina. Recently code-named Cat—our cat burglar.

And Beaker, the Goth chemist, always with different-colored hair—black-and-white-striped this week. She wore a perpetual smirk and never seemed to be in a good mood. And she *always* chewed gum ferociously, like if she didn't, she'd explode or something.

"Well?" prompted Wirenut.

Screw keeping everything a secret. I was tired of secrets. I took the lollipop out of my mouth, took a deep breath, and told them everything. About my parents. About Eduardo Villanueva. And that I'd given TL an ultimatum—help me go after my parents' killer or I'd leave the Specialists.

No one uttered a sound when I finished. Mystic, Parrot, and Beaker just stared at me while the others exchanged silent glances.

From their shell-shocked expressions, no one could really believe what I'd just told them.

More time went by, and still no one said anything. Only the faint sound of Wirenut and Cat's iPod filtered through the air.

Finally, Bruiser cleared her throat. "What can we do to make sure you stay?" Her soft tone, so unlike her, made tears press against my eyes.

"Nothing." I swallowed. "TL knows where I stand."

※ ※ ※

bzzzbzzzbzzz.

My cell went off. I reached over to my dresser, picked it up, and checked the display: ***. It was TL's stat code.

Wide awake, I quickly swung my legs over the side of my bed and tiptoed into the bathroom. Since it was five in the morning, Cat, Bruiser, and Beaker still slept.

I washed my face, swished mouthwash around in my mouth, and then tiptoed back across the girls' room. I tugged on jeans and a T-shirt and quietly made my way out.

The long, dark hallway seemed to stretch to eternity as I strode down it toward TL's room. My stomach flip-flopped in anticipation.

Coming to a stop at his door, I closed my eyes and took a couple of deep, fortifying breaths.

This was it. In a couple of minutes, I'd find out if I was staying or leaving. I'd gone over our conversation an endless number of times last night. I felt no regrets for giving TL an ultimatum.

I'd had to do it.

I hoped he understood and didn't make me leave. I loved my new life and wanted more than anything to stay.

Opening my eyes, I tapped on TL's door.

"Enter."

I turned the knob and stepped inside. David sat in one of the metal chairs in front of the desk. What was he doing here?

He didn't look at me as I took the seat beside him. I sensed he was upset about something. He was probably mad I hadn't told him about the ultimatum. I would have, but I hadn't seen him since my conversation with TL.

Behind TL, his bedroom door sat propped open. His covers and pillows didn't appear disturbed.

TL picked up his mug with a tea bag dangling over the side. "I'm going to say this only once, and there will be no more discussion on the subject." He made eye contact with first me and then David. "My marriage to Nalani Kai is no one's business but mine. Neither of you will tell anyone she is my wife. As far as you're concerned, she's a field agent. Nothing more. Do we understand each other?"

"Yes, sir," David immediately answered.

"Yes, sir," I echoed.

It occurred to me then that David had probably gotten in big trouble for telling me about TL and Nalani's marriage.

I chanced a quick look at David, but he still didn't make eye contact with me. I owed him a huge apology.

"GiGi," TL continued, "you've turned into someone I wasn't expecting. I'm not disappointed. Surprised is a better way to describe what I'm feeling. You proved your psychological profile wrong in stepping beyond your comfort zone of reclusiveness, of living inside your brain, of not taking chances unless forced to. I thought one day you might. I'd *hoped* one day you would. I just wasn't expecting it to happen this soon."

I didn't know if I should take his words as complimentary or not, but I remained quiet and kept listening.

"As I mentioned last night, the IPNC has been after Eduardo Villanueva for years. He's managed to squirm his way out of being captured every single time we came close." TL rubbed his fingers over his shaved chin. "As you two already know, the Specialists are now private. We're no longer run by the government, by the IPNC. Legally, we can't go after Eduardo Villanueva unless the IPNC hires us."

TL dunked his tea bag a few times. "I've spent most of the night on the phone with senior IPNC officials. They've agreed to give us the case."

My heart skipped a beat in anticipation. I hoped this conversation was leading to where I thought it was.

TL sat back in his office chair. "They've given us sixty days to find, apprehend, and bring down Eduardo Villanueva." TL picked up a folder and tossed it in my direction. It landed in front of me at the edge of the desk. "Since you're so interested in going after Eduardo, I'm giving you the case. You're in charge. You will be putting together the mission."

"E-excuse me?" He was kidding, right? I didn't know how to put together a mission.

TL's brows lifted. "You heard me. You want to bring down your parents' killer?" He looked at the folder. "There it is. It's all yours. It's this way or no way. This is a challenge, GiGi. It's part of your training. You've boldly stepped beyond yourself and requested my help. Well, I'm helping you by getting the case. Now let's see how you continue to handle that boldness and plan the mission."

I stared at the folder, itching to peek inside. This was what I'd wanted, to go after my parents' killer. But . . . I didn't know how to be in charge.

TL took a long, leisurely sip of his tea. "There are a couple of conditions."

"Conditions?" Why did there always have to be something else?

He put his mug down. "David will assist you in designing and planning the mission." TL looked at David. "Whatever you come up with, make sure you set yourself up as backup from a separate location."

David nodded. "Yes, sir."

I released an inaudible, relieved breath. Good, David was going.

"I will need to see and approve all plans, the budget, and the equipment lists."

I nodded my head.

"You will be monitored every step of the way." TL tapped his eye. "Never forget, I'll be watching you. Even when you don't think I'll be watching, I *will* be watching."

I nodded again. I didn't expect any less.

"And," TL continued, "Beaker and I will travel with you."

"Beaker?"

TL nodded once. "Beaker. She will be your partner on this mission."

Groooan. Anybody but her. She *hated* me. For that matter, I didn't much like her either.

"Make your decision now. Yes or no. What's it going to be? It's this way or no way."

Without hesitation, I slipped the folder from his desk. "Yes."

▦ ▦ ▦

MINUTES LATER, DAVID AND I stood in the hallway at the mountainous mural. He placed his hand on the globe light fixture. A hidden laser housed within scanned his prints, and the mural slid aside to reveal the ranch's secret elevator.

We stepped inside, David punched in his personal code, and the car descended.

Without looking at me, he pulled two energy bars from his back jeans pocket and handed one to me. "Breakfast." Still not making eye contact, he opened his energy bar and took a bite.

I studied his bent head as he chewed, swallowed, and took another bite. He was really upset. Either that or his flip-flops must be real interesting with the way he was staring at them.

"David?"

He didn't look up.

I sighed. It'd been so long since this kind of friction stood between us. It felt awful. And I was the reason why.

The elevator stopped on Sub Four. David reached for the control panel.

"Wait." If I didn't say something now, we wouldn't have privacy later. "I know you're upset."

He took his hand away from the control panel but still didn't make eye contact.

"I'm sorry. I'm really sorry that I told TL I knew about Nalani. You trusted me with that information, and I screwed up. I never intended on saying anything, but I was so mad that it came out before I had time to stop it."

David shrugged a shoulder, still studying his flip-flops. "My fault. I should've known better than to tell you. To tell anybody."

That made it worse. In other words, David couldn't trust me.

But . . . how fair was that? Everyone made mistakes. This one shouldn't mean David suddenly couldn't confide in me.

I reached out and took his hand, hoping he wouldn't pull away.

He didn't, thank God.

"I *am* really sorry. Please know you can trust me with anything. I made a mistake and won't make it again. I promise." I squeezed David's hand. "Was TL really mad at you?"

"He wasn't happy."

Translation: Yes, TL's mad.

David respected and admired TL. Everyone did. But David had lived here for years and had known TL longer than anybody. They had a working relationship, sure, but their friendship was rooted in years of mutual loyalty.

And my uncharacteristically big mouth had come between them. Of all the times for me to get lippy, I had to do it with two people I cared for a lot.

Finally, David brought his eyes up to mine. I saw hurt in their dark depths. "Why didn't you tell me you'd threatened to leave?"

My heart paused. While I sensed he was upset about this when he didn't look at me in TL's office, I was hoping it was just my imagination. "I didn't tell anyone." I shook my head. "Well, I mean, I told my roommates and the guys last night after my meeting with TL."

"But why didn't you tell *me*?"

"B-because . . . because you weren't in our bedroom, I guess. Everyone else was, so I told them. If you would've been there, I would've told you, too." Even to my own ears, my reasoning sounded weak. I should've told David first.

He let go of my hand, and I immediately missed the warm contact. "Reverse the situation, GiGi. What if I'd threatened to leave? Wouldn't you be upset to find out through someone else?"

My shoulders drooped. "Yes." He had a point. I'd feel awful if someone else told me David was leaving. It'd make me feel like he didn't return the feelings I had for him, that he thought our relationship insignificant.

"How do you think I felt when TL told me? I didn't know what to say. I was shocked."

"I'm sorry."

David ran his fingers through his hair. "Do you understand that if any one of us leaves, we're not allowed to have contact with anyone here? If you would've left, none of us would've seen you or spoken to you again. *Ever.*"

I swallowed. "I didn't know. I'm sorry." I'd never thought to ask about such things. I'd never planned on leaving.

He shook his head. "Why didn't you come to me? We could've figured out a game plan. We could've sat down and talked things through. Come up with something other than you leaving. We could've gone to TL professionally. You're lucky he didn't kick you out last night."

"I'm sorry. I was so tired and frustrated and . . . sad." *God,* what had I done?

David punched in his personal code on the elevator panel. "That's no excuse for making rash decisions. If you've learned anything in the Specialists, it should've been that."

I threw my hands up. "I'm sorry again." What else could I say? I'd made mistakes, but everything turned out all right. I got to stay here at the ranch, and we were going after Eduardo Villanueva.

He stepped off the elevator. "Stop apologizing. It's getting on my nerves."

My jaw dropped.

David took off down the hall.

"Everyone makes mistakes," I called to his back. "You're not perfect either. I can't believe you're this mad at me."

He whipped around. "Yeah, I'm mad. I spent months telling myself I liked you only as a friend. And when I finally admit there's something more, you almost up and walk away without any thought to it."

"But I didn't walk away. I'm still here." *He'd spent months?*

"You know what I mean." He turned and stalked off down the hall again.

"David." I jogged to catch up. "This isn't about you. It's about my parents. It's about finding their killer." If anybody understood that, it should be him. It wasn't too long ago we were after his father's kidnappers.

"I know. Believe me, I know." He stopped at the computer lab door. "Listen, I need time to think. I need time to cool off. And you've got a lot to deal with. Let's just focus on the mission."

I preceded david into the computer lab with a mix of emotions swirling in my heart. I'd hurt and disappointed him with the decisions I'd made. And even with that, he still admitted he liked me. He'd told me that before, but this time it seemed to come from his soul.

I just hoped things could go back to the way they'd been.

The computer lab door suctioned closed behind us, making a cool swooshing noise straight out of a sci-fi movie.

David headed to the coffeemaker in the far corner. In the sink beside it, he poured out Chapling's thick muck, cleaned the pot, replaced the filter, and started a fresh pot.

I crossed the tile floor to the four computer stations that formed a square. One was mine, one was Chapling's, and two sat vacant. I sat down at my station, taking in my setup. Wide, flat screen. Wireless keyboard and mouse. Made to order to my specifications. Too good to be true. I loved my computer.

I placed the case file TL had given me next to the keyboard and touched the mouse. A dancing cartoon screen saver of a red-headed little person—courtesy of Chapling—flicked off. I keyed in my password.

HELLO, GIGI, Daisy, the ranch's system, greeted me.

"Hi, Daisy," I greeted her back.

"Shhh," David hushed me, and I glanced over at him.

Chapling, he mouthed, pointing behind the standing metal cabinets that bordered the right side of the lab.

Pushing back from my computer, I shuffled over and peeked around the end of the cabinets. Chapling lay on the floor in the corner, curled up in a chubby little ball. His tools and the guts of a computer were scattered all around him.

He inhaled a soft snore, and I smiled. I'd never seen him sleep before. Actually, I'd never seen him so quiet and still. Guess the caffeine finally drained out of his system.

David waved me over to the computer stations and, rolling out a chair, sat down at a vacant station next to mine. "Let's be as quiet as possible," he whispered, "so we don't wake him."

Nodding, I sat down behind my computer.

David pointed to the energy bar I'd shoved down my front jeans pocket. "Eat that, please, before you forget and hours go by and you still have nothing in your system."

"Sorry," I mumbled, taking out the energy bar. For some reason, eating was one of those things I rarely remembered to do. If it weren't for David and my friends, I'd probably eat once a day, if that.

I opened the package and took a nibble.

David pivoted his black leather chair toward me. "Before we get started on the mission planning, I need you to listen closely to what I'm about to tell you."

Swallowing my bite, I pulled my notepad from my back pocket and slipped the miniature pencil from the spiral. "Okay, shoot."

He gave the notepad a quick look.

I frowned. "What?"

David's lips twitched. "Nothing."

I narrowed my eyes. He better not have anything to say about my dorky notepad.

"Okay." David rolled his chair a little closer. "This is one of the best, yet most difficult things TL has ever taught me."

I nodded, focusing.

"You have to remove yourself emotionally from a mission. Personal feelings muddle rational thinking and effective decision making. Remember the Ushbanian mission? My father was being held hostage. Talk about emotional disruption." David tapped his head. "Find a place in here to keep your emotions separate. Otherwise, they'll mix and mingle and affect rational decisions."

I remembered the Ushbania mission. "When TL first presented the mission to us, you thought it was best you didn't go." That must have been so hard for David, knowing his dad was being held hostage.

David nodded. "That's right. When all I really wanted to do was storm over there and kick some butt."

And to think he'd been in such control. Calm. Focused. "You did great."

He smiled a little. "Thanks. Which brings us to you. *Your* parents are involved this time around. As hard as it is, you have to emotionally separate yourself. Look at the mission objectively, as though it's someone else's family, not yours."

I blew out a breath. "That's going to be *extremely* difficult."

"Yes, it is. But you can do it. You'll *have* to do it in order for the mission to succeed." He rolled his chair out and stood. "Coffee's done brewing." He pointed to my energy bar. "And you need to finish that."

While he poured the coffee, I quickly ate the rest of my energy bar. As I chewed, I slowly clicked my brain into mission mode, compartmentalizing my personal emotions away from logic, just as David had suggested. It didn't work so well, though. I couldn't get my mom's smile out of the forefront of my mind.

He placed a mug beside my notepad. I took a sip. Mmm, exactly the way I liked it. Lots of sugar and no cream.

It occurred to me then that I'd never told David how I liked my coffee. He must have watched me make a cup, and remembered.

He put down his mug and took his seat. "First thing we have to do is scan through Eduardo Villanueva's history and then find out where he'll be next. Once we find out where he's going to be, we'll study the area and build our cover around that."

David took the folder from beside my keyboard. "Let's review the case file and familiarize ourselves with Eduardo and his affairs."

I watched as he scanned a page, then flipped it and perused another. "Looks like he was born into the business. His father and grandfather had their fingers in all sorts of things." David turned another page. "Eduardo's brothers, sons, and nephews are all involved. One branch of the family tree handles drugs, another guns, and our guy, of course, smuggles chemicals." He shook his head. "One big, dysfunctional, happy family."

"What about the women?"

David quickly read, shuffling through papers. "The women have the children and stay home, supporting their wealthy crime husbands. The entire family lives in South America."

"Interesting," I commented.

"I'm going to keep browsing through this. You see what you can find out about his next operation."

With a nod, I took a long, sugary sip of my coffee. Staring at the blinking cursor on my black screen, I let my brain click through its processes and organize a plan to trail Eduardo's transactions, which would lead me to his network and personal computer. From there I'd hack and be in.

I picked my glasses up off the table and slipped them on. I placed my fingers on the keys, and they suddenly flew. I cross-connected networks to cover my tracks. I wove in one grid and out the next, then leap-frogged through satellites. I ran an interpretation program to translate Spanish to English and located Eduardo's last bank transaction three days ago in Venezuela. I created an algorithm to sneak in.

A few more clicks and . . .

ACCESS DENIED.

Hmmm . . . *click, click, click* . . .

ACCESS DENIED.

Huh . . . *click, click, click* . . .

ACCESS DENIED.

Okay, think, GiGi. What's the most important thing to Eduardo? Chemicals? "Do you have a list of the chemicals he's smuggled in?"

David flipped some pages in the folder and pulled out one. He handed it to me. "Two sided."

I ran my gaze down the three columns of substances and flipped it over to see just as many. Randomly, I picked out a dozen and typed them in.

ACCESS DENIED. ACCESS DENIED. ACCESS DENIED.

On and on I typed chemicals as passwords. And one by one my access was denied.

With a sigh, I sat back and thought from a different angle. The most important thing to Eduardo obviously wasn't chemicals. David told me Eduardo has a big family and that they live in South America.

I did a quick search on South American countries and cities and tried a few of those.

ACCESS DENIED.

Okay, let's try family. "Give me the birthdates of Eduardo's children."

David flipped a paper, perused. "Six, seventeen, sixty-eight. Eight, five, seventy-one. And eleven, thirty, seventy-three."

I keyed them youngest to oldest first.

ACCESS DENIED.

Then oldest to youngest. ACCESS GRANTED. "Finally, I'm in."

Stupid me. I should have tried family first. Most passwords were derived from relatives' names and dates. You'd think the bad guys would know this and choose something else.

His transactions scrolled across my screen. It came to a stop, and my gaze fell on the last figure. "H-holy cow."

David glanced up from the case file. "What?"

I blinked. "Whatever chemicals he sold in Venezuela made him seven million two hundred thousand dollars. And change."

David whistled.

I shook my head. *Unbelievable.*

He tapped the open folder. "According to this, Eduardo lives in Potasi, Colombia. The only computers inside his mansion belong to his grandkids. All communication from him happens via remote access."

"I figured as much." I clicked some keys. "So let's see if we can find that computer of his."

Click, click, click . . .

ACCESS DENIED.

Staying with the family theme . . . "Give me his grandchildren's names."

David shuffled through the papers. "Wafiya, Arturo, Unice, Ciceron, Sophronia, Emilio, Quetcy, Gaspar, Odette, Ivan, Kemen, Moises."

On my notepad, I jotted down all the names. Twelve in all. Jeez that's a lot of grandkids. "Now ages."

David read those off, too, while I scribbled.

On the Venezuelan transaction, he arranged his kids from

oldest to youngest using their birthdates. So I needed to try the opposite order with his grandkids, using their names.

But passwords can't be more than twenty-one characters long. If he used the first letter of each of their names arranged youngest to oldest . . . quickly, I typed the letters, my blood zinging with the awesome energy that came with figuring out a puzzle.

Bingo. "Got it."

David glanced up. "You're kidding. It's been only," he checked his watch, "seventeen minutes and fourteen seconds since we sat down. I haven't even drunk half of my coffee. And I've thoroughly read through only page five in the case file."

I shrugged. Seemed like it'd been a lot longer. "I would've been quicker if I'd thought of the family angle first."

David smiled and shook his head.

Click, click, click . . . "I'm copying his hard drive." I watched the screen flick. "It's encrypted. I'll work on that in a minute."

David came to stand behind me. "Are we talking everything? As in decades ago?"

I pushed up my glasses, ignoring his cologne drifting around me. "It appears so." My screen continued scrolling. "I'll know for sure when I run this through some of Chapling's decryption software."

As my computer continued copying, I started processing batches of the data through various decryption programs. I tried a standard alpha-numerical package first, then a beta platform. I ran it through a transcendental process, and slowly the encrypted data became readable.

"Here we go." Suddenly, a thought hit me. "Wait. If this is everything, then we have him. We have evidence. He can be arrested as soon as right now."

The screen stopped scrolling. David reached to my right, and, using my mouse, he clicked through the decrypted files, opening random ones and quickly scanning them. "What we have, essentially, is a journal. Yes, it chronicles everything he's had his fingers in, but TL will tell you Eduardo has to be caught in the act."

David let go of my mouse. "So we need to figure out where he's going to be next."

While I continued to click away with the files, weaving through Eduardo's hard drive, David resumed his seat. He flipped a page in the case file and continued studying.

"Barracuda Key," I announced, looking at a satellite map of Florida that popped up on the screen. "It's one of many tiny islands trailing off the southern tip of Florida."

David rolled his eyes up from the file. "Do you realize I've read exactly one and a half paragraphs?"

I shrugged innocently. "Do you want me to work slower?"

He sighed through a smile. "No, of course not. Sometimes I forget what a genius you are." He closed the file. "Barracuda Key?"

I nodded.

"What's going on in Barracuda Key?"

I started searching his journal again. "Let me see"—*click, click, click*—"Huh"—*click, click, click*—"Oh my God"—*click, click, click* . . .

David rolled his chair over. "What?"

"He's not just smuggling in chemicals." A few more clicks. "According to this, people are actually going to Barracuda Key to get these chemicals and make their own bombs on site. Then they'll be shipped out from there." I rubbed a tight muscle in my neck. "So what's next?"

"Find out when he's going to be in Barracuda Key."

Click, click, click . . . "In four weeks."

"Where's he staying?"

"Give me a minute." I pulled up all the hotels in Barracuda Key and hacked into their systems, cross-referencing phrases in Eduardo's journal. "From what I've been able to gather, the Hotel Marquess."

David rolled his chair closer to see my screen. "Now bring up every tourist function and event going on in Barracuda Key, Florida. Preferably at the same hotel. We have to find your cover. You can't just show up as a vacationer. You have to blend in with a group. We need to have a reason for you being there."

"Makes sense. Let's see . . ." I went to the tourist Web site for Barracuda Key island and began searching. "Boy Scout Jamboree?"

David shook his head. "Won't work with Beaker. It'd work if TL wanted one of the guys to go."

"Why *is* Beaker"—I tried not to cringe as I said her name—"going?"

"I thought that was pretty obvious with the chemicals involved." David's eyes crinkled. "My other guess is because you two don't like each other, and everyone knows it. This is TL's way of making you two get along."

"Beaker doesn't like anyone," I defended myself. "It's not about me not liking her. I like her all right." Who was I kidding?

"Mmm-hmm. Right."

I narrowed my eyes.

"Back on track." David pointed to the screen. "What else?"

Click, click, click . . . "Elderly lawn bowling tournament?"

"No. Let me see." He took my mouse and scrolled through Barracuda Key's Web site and upcoming events.

"Heeeyyy," Chapling yawned, stumbling out from behind the metal cabinets.

I smiled, seeing his red, Brillo pad hair lying in clumps, some flat to his head, others sticking straight out. "Morning, Sleeping Beauty."

He yawned again on a stretch, reaching his stubby arms toward the ceiling. His T-shirt rode up over his pale, pudgy stomach. He blinked a few times and yawned once more. "One of you two kids made coffee." He inhaled loudly. "I smell it."

While David continued clicking through the Web site, Chapling poured a cup and wandered over.

He took a sip. "Little weak."

I gave him a sympathetic look. "David made it."

"Ah, that explains it."

David shot him a playful glare.

Chapling took another sip. "TL says we'll be hacking into Eduardo Villanueva's computer today."

"I already did."

He rubbed his bloodshot eyes. "Let me get a little more java in me and we'll— Wait . . . what'd you say?"

I lifted my brows. "Already did it."

He sighed. "Why do I come to work anymore?"

I didn't bother reminding him he never left work.

He circled around me and climbed up onto his chair. "Smartgirlsmartgirl. Course, with a little bit of time," Chapling muttered, "I would've figured out how to hack in, too."

"Of course," I agreed. Chapling was, hands down, the most intelligent person I knew. I'd learned a lot from him.

"Got it." David stood up. He pointed to my computer. "I found yours and Beaker's cover."

I narrowed in on the screen, and my eyes widened. "Uh-uh. Forget it. There's no *way* I'm doing that. There's no way *Beaker* would do that. You've got to be crazy. No." I shook my head. "No. No. No. No. No."

4

AFTER AN HOUR of David's trying to convince me this cover would work, reluctantly—let me repeat that—reluctantly, I went with his idea. But I was seriously dreading presenting it to Beaker tomorrow morning.

Putting that aside, David and I spent the rest of the day designing the Barracuda Key mission. He taught me how to view everything omnisciently and then step into the mission and go through the different scenarios we might encounter.

The entire process was incredibly involved, detailed, and organized. It amazed me that TL went through this every single time. But that was his job as the strategist, in charge of planning and implementing the missions, as well as keeping all of us Specialists in line. A lot of pressure came with designing a mission. If something went wrong, then all the blame fell on the strategist's shoulders. In this case, that would be me.

Frankly, the whole process wore me out. And made me admire TL even more.

It was late when we finally finished putting together the mission. Then I practiced presenting it over and over again while David watched and gave input.

Now it was early morning, and here I sat in the conference room. David was across from me, calmly waiting on TL's arrival.

Beside me, Beaker slumped in her chair, chomping on yet another piece of gum. "Don't know why you can't just tell me why I'm here."

I studied her ever-present sour profile while she scowled at the wall behind David. She was going to be *so* PO'ed when she found out our cover.

"What are you"—*chew, snap, chew*—"staring at?"

How beautiful you are, I wanted to snide, but instead asked, "Why do you chew so much gum? It's not good for your jaws, you know."

She slid me a sideways smirk. "Anything else, O Gifted One?"

My nostrils flared. I couldn't recall ever having that reaction to anyone before. Then again, Beaker brought out the worst in me.

The door opened, and we turned to see TL step in.

He nodded. "Good morning. Glad to see everyone's prompt." He took his seat at the head of the table and placed a small, thin box in front of him.

I recognized it. It held the monitoring patches we were each given months ago when we first arrived. The patches allowed TL to track us, to know where we were at all times, and to monitor our conversations. But when he felt confident we'd settled into our new lives, he took them away.

He'd taken mine right before the Ushbanian mission, and he'd taken Wirenut's before Rissala. Which meant TL was probably about to take Beaker's.

"Beaker, you have proved adept at your cover. You've learned how to go throughout your day-to-day activities smoothly, naturally, and without a second thought. You've seamlessly merged into this new world."

TL had said the same thing to Wirenut and me, too.

"It's time for you to take off your patch." TL removed the lid and slid the box toward Beaker. "Place it in here, please."

For a few seconds, Beaker stared at TL and didn't move. Didn't even chomp her gum.

She moved her eyes off TL to me and then over to David. I'd never seen her so vulnerable, so full of disbelief, so . . . stunned. I had the unnerving urge to hug her or something.

Gradually, she resumed her gum chomping and pushed away from the table. She leaned over, pulled her baggy pant leg up, and, from the underside of her knee, peeled away the bandage looking device.

She dropped it in the box and slid it back toward TL.

He nodded. "Congratulations."

Beaker lips curved. "Thanks."

He got up and opened the door. "You three come with me."

Filing out behind him, we followed TL around the glass-paneled, high-tech workroom and down the hall with all the locked doors.

I'd bet my next lollipop TL was about to show Beaker her personalized workroom. He'd given me access to the computer lab after taking my patch, and he'd given Wirenut access to the electronics warehouse after taking his.

If history repeated itself, Beaker was about to get the surprise of her life.

At the end of the long hall, we stopped at a steel door that had a large hole in the center.

TL turned to Beaker. "This is your room. You can come and go anytime you want, unless you're expected to be somewhere else. No one has access to this room but myself, you, Chapling, and David."

"Why Chapling?" I asked.

"Chapling has access to everything. He monitors the whole ranch." TL pointed to the hole. "Beaker, insert your hand as a fist. When you're inside, spread your fingers as wide as they'll go. You'll feel a flash of ice and then immediate warmth. It will not hurt. Make sure you *don't* flinch."

"Ice and then warmth? That's blumeth and parabendichlor." Beaker put her fist in the hole. "You're chemically reading all five of my prints."

One side of TL's mouth lifted. "Very good. As soon as you remove your hand, immediately step back from the door."

Beaker slid her hand free, took a quick step back, and the door dropped straight down into the floor.

I jerked. Sheesh, that was quick.

TL stepped through the opening, and we all followed. He showed Beaker a flat, silver disk on the wall next to the opening. "This operates the door from the inside." He pressed it, and the door whooshed back up, making my hair fly sideways.

Turning, I surveyed the room. Of course, I knew next to

nothing about chemistry, but this looked pretty darn cool. And if Beaker's wide-eyed expression held any indication, she thought so, too.

As she began slowly wandering around the room, I took in the details.

Tall, see-through glass-front wood cabinets bordered the right side, with all sorts of jars, bottles, tubes, and flasks. It seemed like hundreds of them lined the cabinet shelves. A variety of substances filled them: liquids, powders, roots, stems, moss, granules . . . so many different colors and things it was impossible to take it all in.

Matching see-through cabinets bordered the left side of the lab, with dozens of different tools: burners, scales, thermometers, scissors, bowls . . . again, so much it was impossible to take it all in.

A closed metal cabinet labeled SAFETY GEAR sat along the back wall with a few sinks and even a shower beside it. I supposed a chemist would need a shower in case something went wrong with all the dangerous chemicals.

A contemporary stainless steel refrigerator occupied each corner of the room. Four long, black, granite-topped tables lined the center, with tall stools underneath. Equipment dotted the back two tables. I recognized the microscopes, but I was clueless about the rest.

I'd never seen anything like this room. The labs in high school and college certainly didn't compare.

Across the space, Beaker leaned over a machine with spindles. Slowly, she turned a knob, studying it.

"What do you think?" asked TL.

Beaker looked up. "Are you kidding me?" She grinned. Actually grinned. "This place rocks!"

We all laughed.

She pointed to the cabinet with all the liquids. "This is like something straight out of my dreams. A fantasy come true. This is unbelievable."

My mind jumped back to the mission I'd done with Wirenut and Beaker's involvement in it. "How did you help out Wirenut and me without this lab?"

Beaker didn't respond. I doubted she even heard me, too involved in exploring her new room. I'd been the same way when TL first showed me the computer lab.

"She didn't need all this," he answered for her. "She already had a lot of the knowledge. Plus her notes and books and, of course, the Internet." Crossing his arms, TL turned to me. "Do you know what makes Beaker such an extraordinary chemist?"

I glanced across the room to where she stood bent over a microscope. I didn't.

Sad to say, I didn't know anything about her. And I hadn't really had a desire to find out. I'd made no effort with her. Nor had she with me. From the first moment we met, we'd clashed, and it had never gotten any better.

"What makes Beaker so unique," TL continued, "are her methods. She can walk outside and gather grass, rocks, and a bird feather, break them down, and combine them in an infinite number of ways." TL pressed the silver disk on the wall, and the lab door whooshed down. "You're privileged to have such a talented young woman on your team. As she is to have you."

I trailed behind everyone as we exited the lab and made our way back to the conference room.

Mulling over everything TL had said about Beaker, I began to see another side to her. A side that didn't surprise me. Every one of us was gifted in our own special way. But I'd been so caught up in disliking her, I hadn't taken the time to comprehend fully her intelligence.

I glanced at her as we entered the conference room and wondered what her life had been like before the Specialists. What had happened to make her the person she'd become?

TL closed the conference room door, and we resumed our spots around the table. He looked at me expectantly, and David handed me the remote control. "All yours."

Taking the remote, I rolled my chair back and stood. Not a single nerve danced in my belly. Only confidence flowed through me. "I'll begin by recapping Eduardo Villanueva's case file."

I detailed every single thing about him, tracing his life from childhood to adulthood. From what school he went to, to the women he married, to his children and grandchildren. I described every man and woman he'd ever worked with. I defined every drug, gun, and crime deal he'd been involved with, and, of course, the chemical smuggling ring.

You name it, I gave the information.

The entire time I spoke, I used the remote control to flash pictures up on the flat screen. I showed images of where he lived, of his kids, of his business partners.

I displayed images of all the men, women, and children he'd murdered. As my parents' picture flashed onto the screen, I tried to keep my emotions in check, but took pause for a second to breathe. Just to breathe.

When I felt ready, I continued, and for thirty minutes I dumped even more information. When I finished, I paused. "Questions?"

Everyone shook their heads.

"This brings us to the here and now. Mr. Villanueva will be in Barracuda Key, Florida, in four weeks. According to intel, this will be his largest chemical shipment yet." I pointed my remote at the screen. "These are the chemicals that we know are coming in. There are five or six unknown ones, too."

Slowly, I scrolled through the list of chemicals. "We're unsure of how they're being smuggled in, where they're being stored, and where his buyers are going to be making the bombs. But we do know where he's staying." I looked at Beaker. "How familiar are you with these chemicals?"

"I've studied them all. Some I've actually worked with. I'll tell you a combination of many of those can blow up a whole city. They can be tweaked, though, and some of those can be used to defuse the others." She scooted up in her chair. "Most of those substances are on timers. In other words, they have to be used in a certain amount of time to be effective. Or they have to be defused in a space of time or they will self-combust."

"Beaker," TL addressed her, "in case you haven't figured it out yet, you will be going on this mission."

She smiled a little. "Yeah, I sort of guessed that."

TL held up his hand. "Let's pause here for a second and go down a different avenue. I want to know who's on the team and what the cover is."

"The team will consist of myself, Beaker, David, Nalani, and you, TL. We'll be staying at the same hotel as Eduardo." I clicked the remote control. "Here at the Hotel Marquess. We'll be able to monitor his moves and track him through that venue. David will be staying at a different location as backup. Nalani will obtain a job at the Hotel Marquess and act as our insider. Here at home base, we'll have Chapling and Parrot on stand-by. We'll need Parrot on call for translations, because Eduardo operates his transactions in a variety of different languages. And our cover . . ." I swallowed, inwardly groaning over what I was about to say.

I took in Beaker's black-and-white-striped hair, her nose chain, green lipstick, dog collar, black baggy clothes, and black nail polish.

I cleared my throat. "Our cover will be cheerleading."

▥ ▥ ▥

THIRTY MINUTES LATER. I was back in my room, and Bruiser was laughing hysterically. "Beaker's going to be a cheerleader? You've got to be kidding me. That's so funny."

I sat on my bed with Cat, both of us trying not to laugh along with her.

"Wait." Bruiser sniffed and held out her hand. "Can't you just see it? Beaker's nose chain in exchange for a *pretty little daisy*." Ha, ha, ha, ha.

"Oh *my* God," Bruiser made her voice airheady, pulling an imaginary piece of gum from her mouth. "This Bubba Jubba is *so* chewed."

This time I smiled. I couldn't help myself.

"And you"—Bruiser pointed to me—"a cheerleader, too?" She grabbed her stomach. "This is too good."

"Hi," Bruiser did the airhead thing again. "My name's GiGi. That stands for Girl Genius." She flipped a red braid over her shoulder. "I can factor, square, and quadruple any of your cheers."

I rolled my eyes. Bruiser could be such a dork.

She fell back onto her bed laughing and rolling around. "Ohhh . . . ohh . . . oh . . ." She wiped her eyes. "Okay." Sniff. "I'm done now."

Good thing Beaker was still down in the conference room with TL. Or rather, TL requested she stay when she started getting irate about the cheerleading thing. She'd probably have busted Bruiser's lip by now.

Cat chuckled. "Now that Bruiser's done being Bruiser, are you and Beaker joining a squad or what? And what's TL's role in this?"

"Beaker and I are going as a pair. Cheerleaders from all over the nation are meeting in Barracuda Key to try out for America's Cheer. It's a national team. TL's going to act the role of our coach, our choregographer."

Bruiser flopped over onto her back. "Beaker actually agreed to this?"

"Not exactly." I wasn't too thrilled with it either. "That's why she's still down there with TL."

Our bedroom door slammed open, and Beaker stomped in. She railroaded right past me, down the length of our bedroom, and stopped at the bathroom door.

She spun and jabbed her finger in my direction. "I'll *never* forgive you for this." She wrenched open the bathroom door and banged it closed behind her.

Cat and I exchanged a glance.

"Does this mean you're going?" Bruiser sweetly called after her.

The toilet flushed.

5

A COUPLE OF days later, Beaker and I shuffled into the ranch's barn, which would double as our cheer training facility.

"Okay, girls," a short blond woman shouted and clapped her hands. "Front and center."

We crossed the cement floor to where she and TL stood on a large square of mats.

Dressed in a tight warm-up suit, she spread her legs wide and planted her hands on her boyish hips. "My name is Coach Melanie Capri. My purpose here is to get you ready for cheer tryouts in Barracuda Key. You don't have to be experts, but you do have to look like you know what you're doing."

I knew all about this woman. TL had arranged for her to come and train us, and David had briefed me on her background. Melanie Capri. Five feet tall. Exactly 105 pounds. Thirty-five years old, although she looked a lot younger. Cheerleader all throughout middle school, high school, and college. After graduating, she coached high school cheerleading for two years and then joined the CIA. One year later, she transferred to the IPNC, where she'd been ever since.

But the best part? She'd actually traveled with America's

Cheer, the same team Beaker and I would be trying out for. As far as the cheerleading part of this mission, it didn't get any better than Coach Melanie Capri.

She reminded me of Audrey, the modeling coach for my first mission. Not the way Coach Capri looked, but her no-nonsense demeanor. My mind flashed back to that training and all the awkwardness that came with it. If I hadn't had it, though, the thought of this cheerleading preparation would be more uncomfortable for me than it already was.

"America's Cheer," she began, "is a weeklong competition. Every year there are approximately one hundred competitors, fifty teams of two. Generally there are ninety percent girls and ten percent boys. The weeklong competition will be grueling. You'll get up at the crack of dawn and fall into bed late. You'll have team rehearsals, attitude-building activities, group instruction, and physical-fitness training. You'll be judged all week long not only on technique, but attendance, talent, personality, and beauty. No one gets eliminated until the final day, and at that time, they will pick the twenty-one new members of America's Cheer national team."

Crossing her arms over her stomach, Coach Capri surveyed first me and then Beaker. "When's this one getting a makeover?" she said to TL.

Beaker snarled. "*This* one's name is Beaker, and I'm not getting a makeover."

Coach Capri arched a blond brow. "Oh yes, you are, darling, attitude and all."

Beaker rolled an irritable glare toward TL.

He maintained a stony face. "Coach Capri is in charge. Whatever she says goes. I'm behind her all the way."

"Let's start with you taking out that nose thing."

"Excuse me?" Beaker ground out.

Coach Capri smiled humorlessly. "You heard me."

With her jaw clenched so tight I thought her teeth might crack, Beaker reached up, disconnected the chain from her ear, and then slid the hoop from her nose.

I grimaced as I watched the piercing slide through its hole.

Slowly, twirling the chain in the air, she smirked at Coach Capri. "Better?"

Coach Capri grinned. "Yes, thank you. You can give that to TL. You won't be getting it back until after the mission."

Beaker narrowed her eyes.

TL held out his hand, and, after a defiant few seconds, Beaker tossed it to him, and it clanked to the floor in front of him.

Coach Capri cleared her throat. "Pick it up and hand it to him nicely."

Beaker glared at her but didn't move.

"Pick it up and hand it to him nicely."

Beaker stood her ground.

Coach Capri's lips curled up, and something about their sinister tilt said she was about to take Beaker down.

Beaker must have seen it to because she walked over—albeit slowly—retrieved the fallen chain, and placed it in TL's outstretched hand.

"Perfect!" Coach Capri complimented a little too brightly.

Pocketing the chain, TL walked to the corner of the room to observe our training.

Coach clapped her hands. "Now let's pop and lock."

Pop and lock?

Coach strode over to where TL stood next to a portable stereo sitting on the floor. "Luckily, we can skip the fitness conditioning, since you two get plenty of that in PT. We're going to go straight into skills. Popping and locking is the most important technique a cheerleader needs." She pressed the play button on the stereo, and techno music started.

"Listen for the thump in the background of the music," she shouted over the noise. She snapped her arms up to her chest and popped them straight out to her sides. "Notice my joints are locked. No spaghetti arms allowed."

She snapped her arms back in and popped them straight out, this time at a different angle. In and out she went, popping and locking, each time at a different angle. Right arm up, left arm down. Right arm sideways, left arm up. Right arm diagonal, left arm down. Some with her fists clinched, others with her fingers straight.

As I watched, I noticed she executed each snappy movement to the bass thumping of the music.

"Now you two," she instructed, still popping and locking.

Stepping away from Beaker, I tried my first pop and lock and winced.

Coach nodded. "Don't throw your arm so hard, GiGi. You don't want to bruise a joint."

I tried again, and in my peripheral noticed Beaker's halfhearted attempt as she slung her arms into place. Her purposeful difficultness annoyed me, although I fully expected her not to cooperate.

Coach Capri moved closer, and Beaker defiantly continued her slinging-arm routine.

"Beaker," Coach warned.

With a smile, Beaker popped and locked her arms, but once coach turned around, Beaker went back to scowling and being lazy. I was starting to get irritated. Why couldn't she take anything seriously? I glanced over at her again, and her defiant look put me over the edge.

I dropped my arms. "Would you stop being the way you're being and take things seriously? This mission is really important to me. I don't need you ruining it."

"Ugh. Everything's always about you," Beaker snapped back.

Pure angry frustration made me take an intimidating step toward her.

She echoed my step, puffing out her chest. "Problem?"

"Yeah, actually I *do* have a problem. With you."

"I don't know why *you* have a problem. I'm the one who has to make all the changes around here." She took another step toward me. "I'm the one who has to get a *makeover* for this mission."

"Oh, would you grow up? Training and getting made over isn't *that* difficult. Just deal with it."

"Oh, that's right. I forgot. This *is* your *third mission*."

"Girls," TL interjected, walking toward us. "Enough. You are going to have to work with each other on this mission to make it successful. So I suggest you suck it up, get over yourselves, and focus on the task at hand."

Beaker and I eyed each other for couple of long, threatening seconds. Then gradually, without turning our backs on each other, moved back to our spaces.

"Again," Coach Capri commanded, as TL returned to his viewing spot.

I brought my arms up, trying pop and lock, and noticed Beaker's arms took on a snappier technique.

Coach Capri backed away. "Now to the music."

Doing my best to ignore Beaker, I listened intently. I heard the thump, but I couldn't seem to pop my arms to the rhythm. I either snapped a second too early or a second too late.

Coach tapped her ear. "Listen to the beat." She went to the stereo and started the music over.

Tuning everything out, I listened and tried again. I popped too early. I tried again. I locked too late.

Pushing out a sigh, I shook my arms out and cut a sideways glance to Beaker. She didn't seem to be having a problem staying in rhythm, and her smirk said she knew she was better than me.

Coach Capri came toward me. "GiGi, concentrate."

"I am." I thought about telling her I had no coordination. Instead, I looked over to TL, and he gave me an encouraging nod.

I tried again. I popped too early. Again. I locked too late.

Dropping my arms, I closed my eyes and took a deep breath.

My brain zoned in, as focused as when I keyed code. I tuned into the music, absorbing it, feeling it pulse through my body. Letters, numbers, and symbols took form, merging together to the beat. GSLK computer code linked in my mind in the same steady rhythm of the techno's bass.

<6E 74 3E 20 78 66 72 6D> Pop.

<3B 0D 0A 69 6E 74 20 6A> Lock.

<3B 0D 0A 66 6F 72 28 6A> Pop.

<3D 30 3B 20 6A 3C 31 30> Lock.

"Good, GiGi," TL complimented.

Opening my eyes, I smiled and snapped my arms into their next position. I *would* get through this training . . . and deal with Beaker.

▦ ▦ ▦

ᴇᴠᴇʀʏ ᴅᴀʏ ꜰᴏʀ ᴛʜᴇ ɴᴇxᴛ ᴡᴇᴇᴋ. Beaker and I woke up early to do homework, went to school, came home, and immediately began cheer training. We were now masters at pop and lock as well as handstands, clapping, and shouting cheers at the top of our lungs. It never would have occurred to me that people needed to practice clapping and shouting.

At night, David and I would meet in the lab to review things for the mission, run budget numbers, and complete any of the dozens of minute details involved. He'd update me on the tasks he was doing to help the mission run smoothly, like completing the enormous America's Cheer registration pack.

And while Beaker still held no excitement about the upcoming mission, today she was downright pissed. Leaning back against the bathroom vanity, I eyed a very snarly-looking Beaker staring at a very eager Coach Capri. Today was makeover day and, clearly, Beaker was not happy about it. Then again, she was never really happy about anything.

Coach Capri dabbed a cotton ball with makeup remover and came toward her. "I don't know how you can see through all that black gunk on your eyes."

Beaker slapped her hand away. "I like my *black gunk*."

"I take it you're not going to do this by yourself?"

Beaker smirked. "You take it right. If you want it done so badly, you do it."

Coach shrugged. "Very well." She grabbed Beaker's wrist, twisted it behind her back, and smooshed the cotton ball across her right eye.

Beaker jerked away, leaving a black mark smeared across her cheek. "Hey!"

"Well, if you'd hold still."

Beaker jerked away again. "Let me go."

"You going to do it yourself?"

"No," Beaker snapped.

Coach Capri backed her up against the bathroom wall. For such a little woman, she was very strong. And her drill sergeant personality made her seem six feet tall.

Holding firm to Beaker, Coach cleaned her eye while Beaker rolled her head, trying without success to dodge Coach's efforts.

"Get me another one," Coach said to me.

Quickly, I sopped another cotton ball with the remover and handed it to her. Beaker shot me a deadly look. I wanted so bad to laugh, but I held it in. She was purposefully being difficult, as usual. And a big, huge, giant baby.

Still holding Beaker, Coach cleaned off her other eye and then let her go. "See. Was that so bad?"

Beaker growled.

Coach Capri didn't even seemed fazed. "Now hair."

"What?!"

"You heard me." Coach picked up a bottle of color. "You can't look like a skunk if you want to fit in at America's Cheer."

Beaker dodged for the door.

Coach intercepted her. "GiGi, lock us in from the outside."

I rolled my eyes at the ridiculousness of the situation. "All right. You two have fun."

Beaker cursed.

I left, locking the door from the outside at the same time someone tapped softly on our bedroom door. Bruiser tiptoed over and peeked out.

"Shhh." She put her finger over lips, shushing whoever stood on the other side.

Cat and I exchanged a "what's up?" look.

Bruiser widened the door a little, and in crept Wirenut, Mystic, and Parrot. The guys spread out in the room: Mystic cross-legged on the floor, Wirenut next to Cat, and Parrot stretched out on Beaker's empty bed.

A muted crash came from the bathroom, followed by a stream of curses.

Bruiser suppressed a giggle.

Coach Capri was one little woman I did *not* want to mess with. I was scared of her, and I wasn't ashamed to admit it. If she snapped an order, I hopped to it. Beaker, on the other hand . . . They went head to head over everything. Literally. From Beaker's clothes, to her oh-so-pleasant demeanor, to her gum chomping, to the way she walked. Coach Capri got in her face about everything.

A bang rattled from the bathroom, shaking the door. Another stream of curses followed.

Everyone in the bedroom exchanged an "oh no" look.

Beaker was going to be so upset when she found all the guys in here. I almost felt sorry for her.

Almost.

More banging, rattling, and yelling came from the inside, while my teammates giggled on the outside. A half hour later, a blow dryer kicked on and minutes after that the bathroom door opened.

Coach Capri emerged. Clearing her throat, she smoothed her short hair into place. "Well, everyone's here. Good." She smiled a little *too* sinisterly. "*Real* good."

In the short time I'd known her, I'd gotten the impression she enjoyed her battles with Beaker.

"You can come out now," Coach Capri called.

Nothing.

"You can come out now," she called again, her voice a bit harder.

Nothing.

"Get your butt out here," she barked. "Now."

This time I held in a giggle.

The bathroom door slammed open, and Beaker stomped out. My jaw dropped. Beaker had gone through a complete transformation. Like an I-wouldn't-recognize-her-if-she-walked-up-to-me-on-the-street kind of transformation. Her hair was colored dark chestnut brown, and it lay in short, layered, loose curls.

She wore very little makeup, and I noticed for the first time her clear blue eyes. With all the overpowering dark eyeliner she usually wore, I'd never seen beyond it to her natural color.

No nose or eyebrow jewelry existed. And even though I couldn't see, I was sure Coach Capri made Beaker take out her tongue stud and belly ring.

I couldn't believe I was looking at the same person. Beaker looked . . . sweet—a word I never thought I'd associate with her.

Her red cheerleading vest, the same as mine, stopped right above her belly button. Her red-and-white miniskirt came to her upper thighs, revealing white legs, and red-and-white tennis shoes completed the outfit.

Other than her pale legs and the frown on her face, she looked beautiful—another word I never thought I'd associate with Beaker.

She scowled at each of the guys, and then her gaze immediately narrowed in on Bruiser.

Bruiser blinked innocently.

Coach Capri slapped Beaker on the back. "It's a good thing everyone's here. You've got to get used to being around people in your new identity."

"Hey, Beak." Wirenut popped a piece of candy in his mouth. "Chin up, babe. You're hot. Who would've thought you had all those goods under your Goth getup."

With a laugh, Cat poked him in the ribs.

Beaker blushed. Actually blushed. I'd never seen her embarrassed before.

"Sissy," Coach Capri addressed Beaker by her real name. "Cheerleaders never frown. Smile, please."

"What's Sissy short for?" Bruiser asked, getting off topic.

Beaker shot Bruiser another scowl. "Priscilla. My mom was an Elvis fan."

Elvis fan? Huh. I hadn't known. I was sure there was a lot about Beaker that I didn't know.

She pointed her finger at Bruiser. "But call me Priscilla, and I'll poke your eyes out."

Bruiser held up her hands.

"Cheerleaders never frown," Coach Capri repeated herself. "Smile, please."

Beaker's ever-present scowl became scowlier, if possible.

Coach Capri arched a blond brow.

Beaker huffed out a sigh. She stretched her lips away from her teeth, looking more like a dental patient then a smile.

Everyone in the room held in a laugh.

Coach Capri cleared her throat. "I said smile, please."

"I am smiling," Beaker hissed through her stretched lips.

Coach Capri bopped her in the back of the head, and Beaker's forced expression curved into an actual smile.

Wirenut tossed another chunk of candy in his mouth. "Now if you could just stay that way and not open your mouth . . ."

Cat bopped *him* in the back of the head this time.

Beaker flipped him a black-polish-free middle finger.

Wirenut rubbed the back of his head. "There's the mad chemist I know and love." He winked.

Bruiser jumped up on her bed. "Let me see you do a cheer." She lifted her left leg from behind, grabbed her foot, and brought it all the way above her head.

I grimaced. From all the cheerleading books I'd been studying, I knew that was called a scorpion—definitely a move I wouldn't be doing on this mission.

"Give me a B!" Bruiser shouted.

Coach Capri arched a brow at me. I knew that arch. I didn't mess with that arch.

Immediately, I pushed off my bed and snapped straight into a liberty, with my right foot on the inside of my left knee and my arms straight up. It should be called the stork the way it looked.

"Give me a B!" I shouted louder than Bruiser.

Coach Capri nodded her head once in a show of approval. Then she turned to Beaker and arched her do-it-now-or-else brow.

With slumped shoulders, Beaker slung her right leg into the same position as mine and flopped her arms up. "Give me a B," she said with all the enthusiasm of a slug.

Coach Capri bopped her in the back of the head again.

I sighed. Here we go again.

▦ ▦ ▦

A WEEK LATER. DAVID AND I stood in Beaker's lab. The large tables were filled with burners, beakers, and vials of various chemicals.

Beaker propped goggles on top her head. "I've been studying all the chemicals Eduardo has used in the past and what we currently know he will be smuggling in. I'm only one person, and I'm definitely going to need help diffusing things when we get to the final hour."

She handed David and me each a thin pack of stapled pages. "I've put together all the various combinations I think will be used in making chemicals bombs. As you can see, I've detailed what to add to various solutions, what to take out, which to heat, ones to chill . . ."

As she continued describing her papers, I looked them over . . . and was suddenly intimidated. She'd used symbols I recognized from high school chemistry and thoroughly explained each one.

She'd expertly noted how many millimeters of this, what temperature of that. She'd organized which stir rods, whisks, and other things to use. But the brilliant detail overwhelmed me. I knew she knew her stuff—after all, this was her specialty—but the sheer magnitude of her knowledge boggled my mind.

Beaker nodded to the table in front of David and me. "Slip on those lab coats and goggles. I'm going to walk you through how to read my notes and defuse a chemical bomb."

"Wh-what?" I blinked a few times. "D-did you say defuse a chemical bomb?"

She smirked a little. "Scared, GiGi?"

I narrowed my eyes. "No. I'm not scared." *Yes, I am scared.*

Beaker rolled her eyes. "Relax." She pointed to the flasks of chemicals lined up in front of her. "We're not actually going to make and defuse a bomb; we're just going to go through the motions. So you know how to read my directions during the real event."

David and I put on our gear while Beaker brought her goggles down to cover her eyes.

She turned on a flame under a flask of yellow liquid. "Refer to scenario one. We'll use that for the purpose of demonstration."

Beaker checked her watch, then turned the flame up a little higher. "Notice in scenario one you have a simple combination of creino and oteca."

"How will we know if its creino, oteca, or any other substance?" David asked.

"You won't know. That's my job. I'll perform some quick tests, tell you what's in the bomb, and you'll refer to the outlined scenarios to defuse it."

"What if there's no time to do the quick test?" I asked.

She shrugged. "It's no big deal, really. It won't take me long to figure out what's in the bombs. If you have any problems, I'll be right there. Don't freak out or anything."

"I'm not freaking out." *I am freaking out.* I mean, what happened if I didn't defuse it correctly? Oh, yeah, it's a bomb. It would *explode*!

Beaker checked her watch again and put two drops of a purple liquid into the now-boiling flask of yellow. "Okay, in scenario one, it says to do what to defuse this bomb of creino and oteca?"

My heart kicked a little. "I thought you said you weren't making a bomb."

With a sigh, David looked at me.

I returned his look. "What? I'm just asking."

"I'm *not* making a bomb." Beaker rolled her eyes again. "Do you not think I know what I'm doing? This would have to reach a *much* hotter temperature before it actually became bomb-worthy." She pointedly looked at the flame. "Of course if you don't tell me how to defuse this, it *will* be hot enough to become bomb-worthy."

I quickly referred to the papers. "It says to take it to at least negative five degrees Celsius within two minutes."

With a nod, Beaker slid over a capped bottle filled with tiny green crystals. "Six of these diumfite crystals will immediately drop its temp to negative five."

She extinguished the flame from the boiling soon-to-be bomb and inserted a thermometer. She dropped six tiny green crystals into the mixture. I watched the boiling liquid turn solid.

Beaker pointed to the thermometer. "Check it out."

David and I scooted in. Sure enough, the thermometer read negative five degrees Celsius.

David smiled. "You are too cool."

Beaker returned his smile, and it occurred to me that I couldn't recall ever having Beaker smile directly at me. "Any questions?"

We shook our heads. With the demonstration, her notes really were pretty simple to follow.

She scooted her frozen bomb to the side. "Now, I wanted to ask you two something. I've been working on a tracking dust that works with a person's DNA. It chemically reacts to their blood. I'm still doing tests, but if I have it ready by the time we leave for Barracuda Key, I'm confident it will be valuable in trailing Eduardo."

David nodded. "We'll have a mission briefing right before we leave. Be ready to show everybody how it works."

Beaker propped her goggles back on top of her head. "It'll be ready. Also, I've developed a powdered GPS compound. It'll last five days in a person's body. I'm calling it crystallized siumcy. I've already told TL about it and he said to talk to you two . . . ?"

David nodded again. "Sounds good. I'm proud of you for being proactive in your thinking and not waiting to be told what to do. That shows real initiative."

She beamed with pride.

He'd sounded just like TL, and David's words had elicited the same devotion that TL's words did. I glanced over at him, swelling a bit with respect and esteem for the guy I liked. If he kept this up, he would be a great strategist one day.

6

WE WERE AT week three of our cheerleading training, and things had gotten tough.

"That was pathetic. That's all you've got?" Coach Capri jabbed her finger toward the barn door. "Go out and do it again. Both of you. You're jogging in here like a computer genius and chemisty whiz undercover on a top-secret mission." Coach Capri widened her eyes. "You. Are. Cheer. Leaders. *Comprende?*"

With a sigh, Beaker and I both nodded our heads.

We're tired, I wanted to whine on behalf of us both. We'd been at this all day long. And a break seemed nowhere in our future.

Turning, we shuffled across the barn and out into a cold, sun-setting evening.

"My project for Excelled Physics is due tomorrow," I grumbled. "And I haven't even started." The story of my life these past weeks.

Beaker stopped to adjust her cheerleading shorts. "I hate these things. They barely cover my ass."

I commiserated. These shorts reminded me of the ones that David had bought me when I first came to the ranch—the ones I had initially refused to wear.

Rubbing her bare arms, Beaker jostled in place. "It's freezing."

"Okay, girls," Coach Capri yelled from inside the warm barn. "Let's see it."

Beaker and I rolled here-we-go-again eyes at each other. In the past few weeks, we'd established a small—let me repeat that—a *small* camaraderie. We definitely hadn't had any heart-to-hearts. But as slight as it was (usually a look or a mumbled complaint), it made things better.

Beaker stepped back into the barn. "Let's do this."

We jogged in, side by side, our feet nearly touching our butts. In my opinion it was a ridiculous way to jog. With our elbows into our sides, we clapped. "H-E-Y. Hey! We're ready for today! P-U-M-P. Pump it up! H-E-Y. Hey! We're ready for today! P-U-M-P. Pump it up! H-E-Y. Hey! We're . . ."

We kept jogging around the barn, grinning, chanting the stupid cheer. According to Coach Capri, at America's Cheer, all cheerleaders would be expected to enter the morning meeting doing this chant.

I didn't see why we couldn't just go in and have a meeting. And why, exactly, did cheerleaders feel the need to spell everything?

"Perfect," Coach Capri yelled over our chanting. "Halt."

"All this peppiness wears me out," Beaker grumbled.

"Okay," Coach said. "TL got called away to a meeting. So David's here to assist with back handsprings." She nodded to the rear of the barn.

From the shadows stepped David.

Inwardly, I groaned. Please tell me he didn't see us.

He passed by us, smiling. "Nice *perky* cheerleading, girls."

Beaker narrowed her eyes.

"We're going to warm up for our back handsprings by doing twenty-second handstands." Coach Capri led the way to the blue mats that ran the length of the barn. "I'll spot Beaker, and David has GiGi."

I groaned. *Again.* Working with David normally thrilled me. But if he was my spotter, I knew where his position would be.

Right in line with my butt. And the shorty-shorts.

Great. *Juuust* great.

At least I'd shaved my legs.

Beaker and I stepped onto the mats. Coach Capri and David were a few feet in front of us.

"Feet together," Coach reminded us. "Point toes. Straight knees. Squeeze thighs. Butt tight. Back taut. Shoulders hollowed. Head neutral. Elbows locked. And arms . . ."

Pressed to your ears, I finished her directions in my head. Coach Capri had said it so many times over the past weeks, I wouldn't be surprised if I mumbled it in my sleep.

Amazingly enough, these handstands came easy for me. Probably because of all the PT conditioning I'd been through since joining the Specialists.

No wonder TL insisted on PT. It made the physical part of training for a mission go much easier.

Now back handsprings on the other hand—I'd yet to nail one.

Beaker and I brought our arms straight over our heads, slid our right toes out, came toward the floor with our hands, and lifted our legs straight up.

Behind me, David lightly grasped my hips.

"Perfect," Coach Capri complimented us. "In sync. Nice job. Now hold for twenty seconds."

I fixed my gaze to a spot on the other side of the barn, concentrating on keeping my body tight, locked, and steady. Trying not to focus on the fact that David's eyes were in line with my butt.

"GiGi, you're not squeezing a penny."

Closing my eyes, I pretended not to hear Coach Capri.

"GiGi, squeeze a penny."

Through my nose I exhaled a sharp breath. *Why me?*

"GiGi, you squeeze a penny now or you're going to hold that handstand for twenty minutes instead of twenty seconds."

Opening my eyes, I glared at that same spot across the barn . . . and then I squeezed my butt cheeks together as if I had a penny between them.

I tried hard to block out what David must be looking at right now. I tried hard . . . and failed.

"Okay, down for ten," Coach instructed.

Beaker and I lowered our right feet and came back to a standing position, our arms stretched above our heads.

I kept my eyes focused on the floor as I waited for the ten-second break. I knew if I looked at David, I'd die of embarrassment.

"And up," Coach Capri said.

We executed perfect handstands again, squeezed a penny, held for twenty, down for ten.

Again and again we repeated it until I didn't think I could hold a penny anywhere.

We brought our feet to the floor, and Coach Capri stood. "Let's take a short bathroom break, and then we're on to back handsprings." She jogged across the barn and out the door.

Beaker grabbed her towel and wiped her face. "I'd better have a good ass after all this is over with."

David laughed.

"I'm going to get some water." Beaker trotted across the barn and out into the night.

Still avoiding eye contact with David, I picked up my towel and folded it. Maybe I should go get some water, too. Or go to the bathroom. Anything to get out of here.

In my peripheral, I saw David.

"Nice pinched penny," he said, looking at my butt and chuckling as he walked past.

I smiled. I couldn't help it.

░ ░ ░

AFTER THREE WEEKS OF TRAINING and preparing, we were ready for the mission. David and I got to the conference room early for the team briefing. I placed a stack of folders neatly in front of my seat, waiting on Parrot, Beaker, TL, Chapling, and Nalani to arrive.

TL had requested that David conduct this meeting as part of

his overall training in becoming a strategist. It felt good knowing David would be in charge. I felt like I was getting a little bit of a break. A lot of pressure came with being the leader. Put that together with training for the mission and going to school, and my life remained beyond busy.

Give me a computer and solitary research any day.

I sat down at my place and let out a long breath, my gaze drifting to the folders stacked in front of me. A folder for every person involved. Every individual who would help me bring my parents' killer to justice.

Slowly, I lifted my finger and trailed it along the spine of the top folder. What if things didn't work out? What if Eduardo got away again? What if, after my hard work, my team's hard work, things still didn't come to fruition? I'd let David down, TL. I'd let my team down. I'd dishonor the memory of my parents.

My parents . . . I closed my eyes as their faces drifted through my head. That time my dad caught a green garden snake and teased my mom with it. She'd giggled and ran around the yard like a crazy woman. And that time they found me hidden behind the couch, waiting for Santa. The tent my dad made out of a sheet. We'd all slept under it in their bedroom. And that ridiculous hat my mom always wore when she cleaned house.

"Shhh." David massaged my shoulders. "It's okay."

Sniffing, I wiped the wetness from my cheek. I hadn't even realized I'd been crying.

I took a couple of deep breaths to clear my head just as the door opened. Beaker and Parrot came in first, taking seats on the other side of the table. Beaker carried a black satchel and set it on the floor at her feet.

"You okay?" Parrot asked me, and I nodded.

Minutes later, TL entered with Nalani right behind him.

Nalani was one of the most beautiful women I'd ever seen. Polynesian, sleek black hair, olive skin, dark eyes. The last time I'd seen her had been during the Rissala mission with Wirenut. She'd driven our getaway boat. In her disguise, she'd had no teeth, greasy hair, and stained overalls.

Now she looked much like she had when I first met her in Ushbania. Very put together and professional. If she and TL ever decided to have children, they would be gorgeous.

Smiling, I got up and gave her a huge hug. "How are you?"

She squeezed me back. "I'm fine."

"How's your job at the Hotel Marquess?" She'd obtained employment weeks ago after David and I had put together the mission.

Nalani nodded. "So far so good."

Chapling waddled in behind her. "I'mhereI'mhere." He glanced up. "Nalani!"

She smiled and leaned down to give him a hug and kiss.

His pale, freckly face turned red. "Oh my. Ohmyohmy."

David closed the door. "Okay, let's get started."

Everyone took seats around the table, and I started handing out folders.

"Beaker, Parrot," David began, "I'd like you to meet Nalani. She's working pre-op on this mission. She's been at the hotel getting things set up."

Beaker, Parrot, and Nalani smiled and nodded to each other.

David began walking around the room. "In two days, myself, TL, Beaker, and GiGi will leave for Barracuda Key, Florida. Eduardo Villanueva, our focus on this mission, will be arriving shortly after us. He's staying in the presidential suite, which is located directly above the room Nalani has reserved for GiGi and Beaker to stay in."

Pointing a remote at the wall-mounted screen, David brought up the hotel's schematics. "These are the blueprints for the Marquess." He zoomed in on a portion. "This is the presidential suite, with GiGi and Beaker's room below. The first objective is to inject his room with DNA dust, which Beaker will describe in a few minutes. This will be done by drilling a small hole into the floor of his room with a silencer."

David zoomed back out. "The second objective is to get an electronic tracker on him. We're taking six different types of trackers, so we'll be ready in any situation. Whether we manage to get close enough in person or are only able to get at him from afar, one way or another we'll get an electronic tracker on him."

He clicked the remote, and different schematics popped up on the screen. "Third objective is to get his room on video surveillance. Notice the presidential suite and the room below share the same ductwork. We'll be using a device Wirenut created called The Fly. It's a mobile camera that can move through the ductwork and into Eduardo's suite through a vent. GiGi will program The Fly to land in an inconspicuous location. And from there, we wait and see where he goes."

David brought up an aerial view of the island. "Barracuda Key is surrounded by the ocean and bordered on the north and south sides by other smaller islands. We don't know how Eduardo is smuggling in the chemicals or how he's shipping out the bombs that will be made. Chapling hasn't been able to decipher that through intel."

Chapling nodded in agreement, as David continued his lecture. "Once we know where and how Eduardo is smuggling the chemicals in, we'll better understand the scope of this operation. He could have three people with him or twenty. Again, something else we've been unable to decipher with our intel. We'll notify IPNC officials once we've organized concrete details, and they'll work in conjunction with us for the takedown. By the time Eduardo has been apprehended, there could be only one chemical bomb to defuse or there may be multiple ones."

David paused and looked around the table. "Are there any questions so far?"

Everyone, including TL, shook their heads no.

David indicated the folders. "Inside you will find complete details of this operation. New identities for me, Beaker, GiGi, and TL; an equipment list; chemical details; miscellaneous logistics; the island layout; travel documents; hotel blueprints and technology; the Marquess's security design . . ." On and on he went, listing things. He pulled the equipment list from his folder and looked at Nalani. "Do you think they'll be any problems getting these things put in place?"

She shook her head. "Not at all. I've already acquired the audio/video monitoring devices. TCVC cable for manually transmitting video from any camera in-house. Socarmi recorders, bugs to plant where we want. Lome cameras to install where we feel necessary, et cetera . . . And I've arranged for a hidden compartment under one of the beds in the girls' room."

She pulled a picture from her jacket pocket and handed it to me. "This is a picture of the bed and headboard. I've had an opening device installed in the headboard's design. You'll notice that there's a shark etched into the headboard. When you bang on its fin, it opens the hidden compartment within the bed."

I studied the picture of the bed. It seemed easy enough.

David turned to Parrot. "You'll need to be on call twenty-four/seven. Intel reports Eduardo operates most often in Spanish and Portuguese, so we may be sending you e-mails or digital recordings of conversations."

Parrot nodded. "I know both those languages very well."

"We won't know the exact combination of substances Eduardo is using until we're there and begin to track him." David pulled a chemical list from his folder. "Beaker has put together a list of all the possible scenarios and how to defuse them. Any changes to this list, Beaker?"

She shook her head. "It's comprehensive."

David switched his attention to Chapling. "Okay. You're up."

Chapling's eyes brightened as he wiggled up a little straighter in his chair. I recognized that look. He couldn't wait to tell everybody about his new software.

"Okay. Okayokayokay. This is way cool." He unclipped his cell phone from his pants. "Now this hasn't been field-tested yet, but I'll get that done before you all leave." Chapling held up his phone. "I've coded in audio software on each of your cell phones that can record anything within a five-mile radius." He giggled. "You can eavesdrop to your devious heart's content as long as you have open air. In other words, you can't record through a wall."

"Tell everybody what you used," I encouraged him.

Chapling bounced his bushy red brows. "A little syntactical code mixed with high-level source data. Then I sprinkled in SPLI mnemonics for good measure." He wiggled his chubby fingers. "Of course, it all has my personal spin on it."

I looked around the table. "Isn't he brilliant?!"

Everybody nodded with one of those confused, yep-sure-I-understood-him smiles.

Chapling pulled on the collar of his shirt, all playfully full of himself. "Well, you know, I do get paid the big bucks."

David nodded to Beaker, indicating it was her turn.

She placed the satchel on top of the table. "I've been working on this for a couple of weeks now. I've run the standard trials and proved it successful." She opened the satchel and pulled out a sealed bottle of red powder. "It's a tracking device that works off a person's DNA. It only lasts for seven days, though." She unscrewed the bottle, took an empty syringe from her satchel, and extracted a full vial of the red substance.

Holding the syringe up, she slowly depressed it. I watched as the red dust turned invisible immediately upon meeting air.

"You don't realize it, but right now this is absorbing through everyone's skin and into their bloodstream." She pulled rose-tinted glasses from her satchel and passed them down the table to TL. "Put those on and tell me what you see."

While he put on the glasses, Beaker pushed back from her chair and began walking around the room.

"Everywhere you move you're leaving a trail of red." TL said, pulling down the glasses. "It's invisible to the naked eye."

Beaker nodded. "No matter where I go over the next seven days, you can track me as long as you're wearing those glasses."

"But if everybody leaves a red trail," I asked, "how do you know who is who?"

From her satchel, she pulled out a small yellow envelope. From the envelope she took what looked like a black toothpick. "Swipe this through the red trail and it'll hold on to the DNA. You can run it through any standard DNA program to see who the trail belongs to. I'll have a DNA kit with us on the mission."

Wow. Neat.

"So what do you think?" she asked, resuming her seat.

David smiled. "Great work, Beaker."

Chapling bounced in his chair. "Oooh, oooh, I wanna try."

Everyone laughed as TL took the glasses off and passed them down the table.

⊞ ⊞ ⊞

LATER THAT EVENING, WITH BOTH HANDS, I grabbed the barn door and slid it open. Stepping inside, I flipped on the dimmer lights. In two days we would leave for Barracuda Key, Florida, and I still couldn't do a successful back handspring. Call me crazy, but I had an issue with blindly flipping backward and falling on my head.

Striding over to the blue mats, I recalled Coach Capri's repeated warning.

You absolutely have to do a back handspring. It's expected of you. You'll be kicked out of the tryouts if you can't. And then your cover will be blown.

Taking mats from the stack in the corner, I spread them down the length of the barn.

I warmed up with a few handstands and then executed perfect cartwheels and roundoffs. I did four front walkovers in a row and repeated going back. All things I couldn't do weeks ago when I'd started this cheerleading training. Not bad for a girl who repeatedly tripped over her own two feet.

Coach Capri should be applauding me for how far I'd come.

Taking off my sweatshirt, I tossed it aside, adjusted my tank top, and went to stand in the center of the mats. I locked my arms straight above my head and took a couple of deep breaths.

I can do this.

Bending my knees, I sprang up and dove backward. I caught a glimpse of ceiling braces, the stalls in the back of the barn, and then splatted face-first onto the mats.

I slammed my fist down. "Oh!"

I laid there, staring at the mat, frustrated beyond belief. Thoughts of my mom and dad began to flood my mind. Did they ever get frustrated at training or had they been naturally good, gifted, at it? Were either of them as klutzy as me? Was klutziness genetic? I shook my head to clear my focus.

"Hey, you becoming one with that mat?" came Beaker's voice.

I glanced up to see her standing in the doorway.

"What do you want?" I pushed to my knees. "I'm not in the mood for sarcasm or jokes."

Beaker shrugged. "I suspect I want the same thing as you, to get some more practice in."

"It's midnight. You're breaking curfew." I stood.

"You're breaking curfew, too."

"True. I'm just surprised you're here. I thought you hated all this cheer training."

"I do." She came the rest of the way in. "Doesn't mean I don't want to be ready, though."

"You don't need to practice. You know how to do back hand-springs."

"And you don't." She stepped onto the mats. "So . . . do you, um, want some help?"

I eyed her for a few suspicious seconds. "Why are you being nice to me?"

"I'm not being nice," she said unconvincingly. She took off her sweatshirt, revealing double-layered tank tops, and tossed it on top of mine. "I don't want you making me look bad at the competition, that's all."

"Mmm-hmm." Well, well, well, could it be that Beaker's actually being nice to me?

She rolled her eyes. "Whatever," she said, and turned to walk away.

"All right." I stopped her. "I'll take any help I can get."

Beaker nodded. "Let's do it," she yelled.

Wirenut stepped through the door, followed by Parrot, Bruiser, Mystic, and Cat.

I sent Beaker a confused look. "What's going on?"

"I rounded up everyone." She shrugged, as if that wasn't the sweetest thing ever. "We're here to help." Playfully, she smirked. "Don't go thinking I like you or anything, though."

I smiled a little. "Of course not."

Wirneut unzipped his windbreaker and threw it aside. "Watch us do handsprings first. Notice we all have different styles. You need to find and do what feels right to you."

Stepping off the mats, I watched first Wirenut, then Bruiser, followed by Cat, and finally Beaker.

Sheesh, was there anyone who *couldn't* do one?

I looked at Parrot and Mystic. They both shrugged.

"We're here for moral support," Mystic offered with a smile.

His smile made *me* smile. What great friends I had.

Wirenut dusted his hands. "Okay, tell me," he instructed, "what did you notice different about all of us?"

"Speed," I answered. "Height. Hand placement."

"It took me five days to learn how to do one," Beaker reminded me.

"You don't have to brag about it," I grumbled.

"My point is," she continued, ignoring my snarkiness, "I would've learned in three if I could've figured out my hand placement. Coach Capri kept telling us to keep our thumbs touching. But when I separated mine by a few inches, I nailed it."

Cat pulled three, long black strips of material from her sweatpants pocket. "Mind giving something a try?"

Eyeballing the black cloths, I shook my head. I'd try anything at this point.

Cat stepped onto the mats and motioned me to follow. She wrapped one of the cloths around my eyes, blinding me. "This is so you won't get distracted by anything." She tightened it. "Don't worry. We're all here to spot you if anything goes wrong."

"Now lift your arms," Cat instructed. She tied my arms tight against my head. "This will keep your arms in place. You'll still be able to flex your shoulders and elbows for the push."

She wrapped the last cloth around my thighs. "There. Now all your body parts will stay where they're supposed to be."

"Remember," Bruiser added. "Reach for the floor with your hands, not your nose."

Someone grabbed my hips and turned me around.

"We're all here," Wirenut spoke from my left. "You can do this."

"Visualize exactly what you want your body to do," Mystic suggested, "and it'll work. I promise you."

Behind the black cloth, I closed my eyes and visualized my body going through the motions of a successful back handspring.

I took a deep breath, bent my knees, and sprang back, diving onto my hands. My palms connected with the floor, and I pushed off, flipping back onto my feet.

I stood for a moment in disbelief. I'd actually done it!

Everyone cheered, and I grinned, literally, from ear to ear.

7

TWO DAYS LATER. dressed in matching red-and-white warm-ups, TL, Beaker, and I boarded the plane. David had already boarded and sat midway in the cabin. As of this moment, none of us knew him. He was traveling to Barracuda Key to do some diving. That was the cover we'd decided on for him. He'd rented a cottage on the other side of the island from our hotel. Once we arrived and went our separate ways, I probably wouldn't see him until the end of the mission.

At least we'd be able to communicate via phone, texting, and e-mail.

As I passed his aisle seat, I slowed, hoping for a slight contact. He surreptitiously reached over and tucked a piece of paper into my palm. My whole body buzzed at the contact.

TL, Beaker, and I found our seats in the back of coach, and after storing our red-and-white backpacks in the overhead bins, we sat down and buckled in. I took a few deep breaths to calm myself—flying was not my favorite thing to do. But I had gotten used to it a little, having had to fly on my first two missions.

Beside me, Beaker raised the window shade. She calmly flipped open a cheer magazine that she'd brought with her and began perusing. I knew she'd rather be reading one of her chemistry books, but we had officially taken on our cheerleading covers when we stepped into the airport.

"Hey," I whispered.

She glanced over.

"Thanks for doing this. It means a lot." I hadn't had a chance to say those simple words to her. "This mission is important to me. And I know you didn't want to go. And well . . . I appreciate all your hard work getting ready for it."

Beaker kept her blue eyes leveled on mine. I got the distinct impression she wanted to say *you're welcome*.

Instead, she shrugged and went back to her magazine. "Yeah, well, I had no choice. TL made me."

I'd like to think it was her way of saying *you're welcome*.

She glanced around me to TL. "Thanks for my send-off party," she whispered.

He smiled a little. "You're welcome."

Beaker went back to her magazine and TL closed his eyes. After a few seconds, I peeked at the note David had slipped me. "I'm right here" was penciled on the inside.

I smiled to myself. He wanted me to know it would be okay. I'd make it through this flight and this mission okay. The loving gesture warmed me.

▦ ▦ ▦

IT TOOK EIGHT HOURS TO fly nonstop from California to the island of Barracuda Key in Florida.

We made our way from the plane through the airport to baggage claim and retrieved our matching red-and-white suitcases.

In the shuttle bus zone, a burgundy Hotel Marquess van waited. Beyond it, I saw David climb into a taxi. Although the windows were tinted, I felt his eyes on me as the cab pulled away.

The elderly bus driver climbed out as we approached. "I take it from your outfits you're here for America's Cheer."

"Yes, sir," Beaker and I answered in unison.

"You guys are the last flight of the day." He took my suitcase first, groaning as he slowly hefted it up into the back of the van. I grimaced at the sound. This little old man was too old to be doing this. He reached for Beaker's suitcase next.

"I got it." She quickly hoisted it into the back before the old man could argue.

TL followed her lead.

I felt horrible. I should've done that, too.

The old man straightened his white uniform jacket. "There was a time when I could've lifted all three without creaking and moaning."

TL slapped him on the back. "No worries. How far is it to the hotel?"

The old driver opened the side door for us. "Straight across the island. Five miles."

With our backpacks, we stepped up into the shuttle van. The driver shut the door, climbed into his side, and pulled out.

Mild, early evening air flowed through the windows as we

zigzagged across the neat and tidy island. I knew from my research that Barracuda Key was five miles wide and only two miles long.

A variety of colorful shrubs and trees filled the landscape, planted at exactly the same distance apart. I didn't know any of the names except for the palms.

We passed shopping centers and grocery stores, all of which stood one-story tall and were painted either beige or white. Brown block lettering on each building indicated the names of the stores or shops. It surprised me not to see any fast-food restaurants.

A black wrought-iron fence surrounded each individual neighborhood subdivision. Inside, the houses had the same one-story, two-car-garage design, and were painted pastel green or pink.

People strolled the sidewalks in perfect, preppy, island outfits.

I supposed Barracuda Key was pretty if you liked the organized, clean, nonunique look.

"Makes me want to pull up a shrub or something," Beaker mumbled under her breath.

"Does the whole island look like this?" I asked.

"Pretty much," the driver answered. "Some of the beach areas are a little deserted, and there's a state park for camping." The driver pointed out the front window. "There it is."

Off in the distance, on what had to be the only hill on the island, stood the Hotel Marquess. Its towering presence came off like an island king looking down over his tropical village.

With huge columns out front, the white-washed hotel stood only three stories tall. The hotel's front and sides covered the entire grassy hillside, and the back extended out on stilts over the ocean.

I knew from my planning sessions with David that the 32,000-square-foot structure housed 449 rooms, nineteen conference rooms, three ballrooms, an underground shopping mall, four restaurants, a spa, indoor and outdoor tennis courts, two pools, an eighteen-hole golf course, and one presidential suite. Where Eduardo Villanueva would be staying.

A person could move into this hotel and never leave. The place had everything.

We pulled up under the portico. Bellmen in matching white-and-burgundy suits emerged, opening the doors, helping us out, getting our luggage.

I couldn't help but feel like a movie star with all the first-class treatment.

A bellman stood on each side of the hotel's entranceway. As we approached, they opened the glass-and-gold doors. "Welcome," they greeted in unison, bowing.

I couldn't recall ever having been bowed to before.

"Thanks," I mumbled, a bit uncomfortable with this royal treatment.

Odd, but this whole place seemed like a foreign country, not a little island off the coast of south Florida right here in good old America.

A slight nudge from TL made me move forward. We crossed through a marbled-floor waiting area. Two more bellmen opened two more glass-and-gold doors. Beaker and I stepped through them and came to an abrupt stop.

In stunned amazement, we stared at hundreds of girls.

Everywhere.

Boinging and bouncing.

Squealing and giggling.

Cheering and chanting.

Tall, short. Skinny, muscular. Blondes, redheads, brunettes. Ponytails, braids.

Wearing a variety of shorts and T-shirts with matching ribbons in their hair.

I'd never seen so many happy, excited, color-coordinated girls in my life.

"Hey!" A dark-haired girl jumped right into our faces.

Beaker and I flinched.

"Isn't this just great?!" she squeaked.

I blinked. Was that voice for real?

"Well, isn't it?!" Her long, brown ponytail swung with her bubbly jostling.

TL put a hand on Beaker's and my shoulders and came up between us. "Yes, it is." He grinned. "You're having way too much fun without us."

The girl giggled.

TL hugged us to him. "Where do we check in?"

The girl snapped her arm straight, pointing across the lobby to the front desk. "Give me an R! Right! Give me T! There!" She spun around and skipped off.

"She could've just said 'right there,'" Beaker grumbled.

"Stay in character," TL whispered and headed toward the front desk through the mass of exuberant girls.

I looked at Beaker, she looked at me, and we both plastered the biggest, fakest smiles on our faces.

With a light spring to our steps, we followed TL across the lobby.

"Hi!" A girl as tall as me bopped up in my face. I stepped back a bit.

"Hi!" Beaker and I greeted her simultaneously. I almost laughed.

The girl's brown eyes widened as she took in Beaker. "Oh my *God*! I *love* your ribbon!"

Beaker's smile became even smilier, if possible. "Thanks!"

The tall girl slammed her hand over her heart. "I *love* how you tied it around your neck. And I *love* how it has little tiny red and white stripes."

Beaker kept cheesing it up, but I knew that underneath lurked her trademark smirk. I could only imagine what was going through her mind right now.

Someone kill this girl and put her out of her misery. No, someone kill me and put me out of my misery.

"Hi!" Another girl danced up.

"Hi!" Beaker and I greeted her.

I wondered how many times I'd have to say 'Hi!' over the next few days.

I purposefully dropped my jaw. "I *love* your T-shirts."

"Thanks!" They answered in unison.

They pointed to their boobs and the green-on-pink lettering stretched across them. "Cheerleaders *are* better athletes!" they agreed with their shirts.

Beaker and I nodded, and I racked my brain for what else I could say.

I love your matching green-and-pink shorts.

I love your matching green shoes with pink socks.

I love your sparkly pink eye shadow.

"Girls," TL called, rescuing me from the dilemma.

"That's our coach. Gotta go. 'Bye!" I gave a quick wave.

"'Bye!" They waved back.

With our huge smiles still in place, we wove through the other joyful girls to the front desk and TL.

He grinned. "Here they are. The next two members of America's Cheer."

"We're glad to have you," the woman on the other side of the counter welcomed us.

Nalani.

Showing no recognition of us, she handed Beaker and me each a big white envelope and card key. "Inside you'll find everything you need. Event schedule, mealtimes, workouts . . . If you need anything while staying here at Hotel Marquess, please don't hesitate to ask."

I glanced at TL to see if I could recognize a hint of love, pain, sorrow, or longing. But I saw nothing except the same fake I'm-so-happy-to-be-here face.

"Unfortunately," Nalani continued, "the room you had been preassigned to is still occupied by yesterday's visitors."

My face dropped a little.

"They decided to stay an additional day. But they've scheduled an early checkout for tomorrow, so we'll have things ironed out in no time."

I glanced at TL, but he was still smiling as if this bit of information was no big deal.

"We'll put you in another room for tonight and then relocate you to your preassigned room in the morning." Nalani pointed down a marble-floored hallway. "Elevators are there. You're in room three-zero-three. I'll let the bellman know where to take your luggage."

TL knuckle-tapped the counter. "Let's go, girls."

Sounds from the lobby faded as we strode down the hall to the elevators. TL pressed the button, and we stood waiting. I was dying to ask him what was going on.

Seconds later, the elevator dinged open and out poured a pack of bubbly girls.

"Hi!" A few of them chirped.

"Hi!" A few more echoed.

"Hi!" Beaker and I returned, our grins in place.

They shuffled by, and we three stepped inside. The door slid closed, and Beaker's smile fell away.

"Ack." She grabbed her throat. "I think I'm going to hurl. This is my worst nightmare come true. Hi!" she sarcastically imitated them. "My name's Pixy, and I don't have a cell in my brain. But I know how to do a toe touch. Woo."

I turned to TL. "What's going on? If we don't get in our room tonight, that means we'll have to wait until tomorrow morning to access the equip—"

TL cleared his throat and shook his head. He brushed imaginary lint from his shoulder. *Stay in character.*

I sighed.

Beaker slumped back against the elevator wall. "I need gum," she grumbled.

TL cleared his throat again, and Beaker rolled her eyes up to his.

He brushed imaginary lint from his shoulder. *Stay in character.* He narrowed his gaze ever so slightly. *Or else.* He rubbed his eye. *Camera watching.*

Smoothing my fingers down my ponytail, I surreptitiously glanced up. Sure enough, in the upper-left corner sat a mini-camera hidden in a speaker. From David's hotel specs, I should've known that, but in my momentary frustration, I'd forgotten.

Reluctantly, Beaker pushed away from the elevator wall. Her scowl inched upward into her rendition of a pleasant face.

The elevator dinged open, and we stepped out. We read the number sign and took a left. Room three-zero-three sat halfway down the hallway.

TL followed us in and shut the door. "Don't worry about the room."

"I know, but I wanted to get a start on figuring out the equipment and reviewing the plans," I said.

"Well, things happen, and plans need to change. We can't control what others do. We'll get you moved into the correct room tomorrow. We'll be a little behind schedule, but not too bad. There's nothing on the cheerleading schedule until tomorrow, so feel free to order room service if you want." He opened our door. "I'm in room three-twelve. See you tomorrow."

"B-Y-E. Bye," Beaker mumbled.

"I heard that," TL called.

He closed the door, and I set my laptop down. "This sucks."

"Yeah, but, oh well. Nothing we can do about it."

Logic told me she was right. But it still sucked.

Tossing down the rest of my stuff, I looked around. A bathroom lay immediately to the left of the door and was decorated with the same gold-and-marble design of the lobby. The shower and toilet each had its own separate little room. Pretty cool.

Farther inside, two king-size beds occupied the majority of the room, decorated with burgundy-and-white comforters and pillows. A long shark had been engraved on each headboard, and, as Nalani said, the fin would release the hidden compartment—in the correct room, of course.

A deluxe wood desk sat in the corner with a brown leather chair in front.

Gauzy curtains covered a medium-size window that looked out over the sun-sparkling ocean.

Matching the color scheme, standard hotel carpet covered the floor.

All in all, it was a great room.

Beaker flopped across the bed closest to the window. "I haven't even been here an hour and my jaw already hurts from smiling."

Mine did, too, actually.

Unzipping the front pocket of my backpack, I pulled out a pack of gum. "Here."

Beaker eyed it warily. "What is it?"

I lifted my brows. "Gum. What do you think it is? Poison?"

She gave me a skeptical look. "Why are you being nice to me?"

Rolling my eyes, I tossed it onto her bed. "Because I'm a nice person."

Beaker snorted, and I turned away, busying myself by reading the Barracuda Key pamphlets on the desk.

Behind me, a wrapper crinkled, and I smiled.

TL and David had done the same thing for me on my first mission, giving me lollipops when I least expected it. It'd always made me feel cozy, comforted, and, well . . . loved.

"Ya know"—*chew, snap, chew*— "you'd think with all the gum I chew, my jaw would be strong enough for the smiling."

It wasn't often Beaker made casual, nonhostile conversation

with me. I turned around, hoping I wouldn't screw up the moment. "Different set of muscle groups."

Staring at the ceiling, she grunted her agreement.

So far so good. "Don't let anybody catch you chewing that."

Beaker blew a huge pink bubble, and it silently popped. "Don't worry. I won't."

I dug around in my backpack, searching for nothing in particular. "So why *do* you chew so much gum?"

Silence.

I dug a little deeper, keeping my hands busy.

More silence.

Great, GiGi. Good job. Way to screw up a rare, sort-of-friendly moment with Beaker.

She sniffed, and I glanced up.

"Um . . ." she started, still staring at the ceiling. "It controls my anger."

Okay. Not what I'd expected her to say. But it made sense with the way she always furiously chomped it. "You must have a lot of anger."

She half laughed. "You have *no* idea."

I found a lollipop in the bottom of my pack. "So what happens if you don't get your gum? Do you explode or something?"

Beaker rolled her head over and looked at me. "Probably."

We both smiled.

She scrunched her face. "Gets pretty bad, actually. I've cussed people out. Hit things."

"Well, remind me to always have emergency gum on hand."

That comment earned a chuckle.

I peeled the wrapper from my lollipop and slipped the black-berry flavor into my mouth. "You should do yoga or something."

Beaker snorted. "Puh-lease." She scooted across the bed, grabbed the room service menu, and began browsing. A few seconds passed.

"Um . . ." she began and then her voice trailed away. "You doing okay? Ya know, with everything's that's going on? Your parents, this mission, blah, blah, blah."

Smiling a little, I sat down in the desk chair. I totally hadn't expected that. Blah, blah, and all. "Yeah, I'm doing okay. Thanks for asking."

She nodded a little and continued studying the menu. "What do you want to eat?" And that question effectively ended our tiny little heart-to-heart.

▦ ▦ ▦

EARLY THE NEXT MORNING OUR room's phone rang. While I scrambled for the phone, Beaker pulled the covers over her head.

"Hullo," I mumbled into the receiver.

"Good morning," Nalani greeted me in her polite, hotel voice. "Your preassigned room will be ready in one hour. The Hotel Marquess is sorry for any inconvenience this may have caused you. Please enjoy breakfast on us."

She hung up the phone, and I fumbled to return the handset to the base. While Beaker grabbed a few more minutes of sleep,

I got showered and dressed and began packing what little I'd taken out for the night. Beaker finally got up and did the same.

We skipped the free breakfast, moved our things to our preassigned room, and began unpacking. I turned on my laptop and connected to the ranch's mainframe right as our door clicked. We both jerked around.

"Lord have mercy!" A petite Asian girl wandered in, talking to someone behind her. "Wait 'til you see this place!"

I looked at Beaker.

What's going on? She mouthed.

I shrugged.

The Asian girl gasped. "Look! The toilet's got its own tiny room!"

"Hello?" I ventured.

The girl spun around. "Hi!"

The girl behind the first girl came up beside her. "Hi!"

I glanced from one small face to the other and then back to the first. Twins.

"We're twins!" They announced.

I smiled. "I see that!"

And I couldn't care less. All I wanted to know was what they were doing here in our prearranged private room, located directly below the one and only presidential suite where Eduardo Villanueva would be staying.

"I'm Lessy!" the first girl introduced, pointing to herself.

"I'm Jessy!" The second girl parroted.

"And we're your roommates!"

8

Beaker and I stayed rooted to our spots, staring at the twin Asian girls with the southern accents.

Lessy and Jessy.

Or was it Jessy and Lessy?

"Did you say roommates?" Beaker asked.

The twins nodded enthusiastically.

I kept smiling while my brain scrambled to make sense of things.

"Sorry." Beaker laughed, covering my silence. "We thought our roommates were going to be someone else," she lied.

Lessy, or maybe Jessy, frowned. "Is there something wrong with us?"

"No." Beaker pushed up from her bed. "Not at all." She crossed the short distance to where the twins stood and stuck out her hand. "I'm Tiffany, and this is my partner Ana," she introduced, using our aliases for the mission.

Still smiling, I remained where I was. I needed to find TL and figure out what our next steps would be.

Beaker cleared her throat, drawing my attention over to her. Without moving her head, she rolled her eyes to the twins.

Oh! I sprung forward and shook each of their hands. "Hi, nice to meet you."

"Make yourselves comfortable," Beaker kept going with the niceties. "We were just on our way out to see our coach."

"Oh, okay!" The twins flopped down on one of the beds. "'Bye!"

"'Bye!" Beaker returned, ushering me out of the room. The door closed behind us. "What is wrong with you?" she hissed.

"I'm sorry. I froze. What are we going to do?"

She tugged me down the hall. "You're not supposed to freeze. You planned this whole mission, remember? If anybody would be allowed to freeze, it'd be me. This is *my* first mission, not yours. And 'What are we going to do?'" She scoffed. "Get it together. I thought you'd be better at this."

She was right. I needed to get it together. It was just . . . well . . . I'd been so thorough during my planning sessions with David, I really hadn't expected anything to go wrong.

Naive of me, I know.

We got to TL's room, and I rapped six quick times—our secret knock. He opened the door, and we slipped inside a room identical to ours.

"My roommate went to get ice," TL fired off. "Make it quick. What do you got?"

Rapidly, I told him the situation while he listened intently.

"What are you going to do," he asked when I finished.

The question caught me off guard. What was *I* going to do? But he always solved the problems. Not me.

"GiGi," TL prompted. "My roommate will be back any second. This is your operation. You asked for this. Now what are you going to do?"

"Text Nalani." I slipped my cell phone from my warm-ups pocket. "We need to meet and find out what's going on."

TL nodded. "Good."

I text messaged Nalani. All of our texts were coded for extra security. She responded within a second. "Third-floor utility closet," I read the display. "Five minutes."

Beaker popped a piece of gum in her mouth.

The door opened, and we all snapped back into role. In walked a guy I assumed to be TL's roommate. He stood a little shorter than me and had neat blond hair. I'd say he was in his early twenties.

"Well, hey!" He grinned. "You must be Ana and Tiffany. Your coach here has been telling me all about you two."

"Hi!" We greeted him in unison.

"Yep." TL squeezed the back of Beaker's neck. "These are my babies. Best girls I've ever had the privilege to choreograph."

Babies? TL would never call us his babies back at the ranch.

He turned to us. "This is my roomie, Coach Luke. He came with the pink-and-green team out of Portland."

The pink-and-green team? That'd be the Cheerleaders Are Better Athletes girls we met in the lobby.

Coach Luke shook his finger at Beaker. "Now, Tiffany. You know you're not supposed to have gum."

With a playful sigh, she rolled her eyes. "Sorry."

Beaker pulled the wrapper from her pocket, squished up the gum, and threw it away. "Won't happen again."

"Well," TL guided us out, "catch you later."

"'Bye!" Coach Luke waved.

"'Bye!" We waved back.

Beaker's smile faded as the door closed. "Do you think these people ever get tired of being in a good mood?"

"Shhh," TL hushed her.

We strode to the end of the carpeted hall and cut a left into the ice and vending machine alcove. The stairwell door sat right beside the utility closest. With a quick glance over our shoulders, we slid inside. The smell of bleach and soap overpowered the tiny space.

Nalani stood waiting, surrounded by bottles and boxes of cleaning supplies. She pulled a small blue pyramid from her uniform pocket and rotated the upper half. I recognized the device from the Rissala mission. Wirenut had developed it. It emitted an inaudible static pulse that blocked others from hearing our conversation.

He'd be so excited to find out Nalani had used it.

Beaker leaned in. "What is that?"

I quickly explained it to her.

"I've got only a few minutes," Nalani hurriedly said. "They think I'm in the restroom. The hotel is packed solid. No vacancy. Your unexpected roommates were last-minute America's Cheer contestants. I didn't check them in; another receptionist did. That's why they're in your room."

"And there's nothing you can do? There's nothing else available?" I asked, almost desperately, even though she'd just said there was no vacancy.

Nalani shook her head. "All the contestants are four to a room. Two to a bed. Your extra bed is the only available one. I'm sorry. If I had checked them in, I would've lied and told them there were no beds, but the other receptionist got to them first."

"What about the room we slept in last night?"

"It's reserved as well."

"And the coaches?" TL asked. "I've only got one roommate."

Nalani checked her watch. "You and your roommate are the only two male coaches. All the rest are women. And, yes, they're four to a room, too. There's no other way. You'll have to work around the situation."

Lightly, Nalani grasped my upper arm. "Eduardo Villanueva checked in a few moments ago."

My entire body chilled as the reality of why we were here hit me. Swallowing, I nodded my head.

With a quick squeeze, she released me. "The equipment is in the bed closest to the wall. Any questions?"

We all shook our heads.

"Wait ten seconds after I leave." Nalani rotated the top of the blue pyramid, turning it off. She handed it to TL. Scooting between us, she opened the door a sliver and peeked out. Then soundlessly, she slipped into the alcove and down the stairs.

Ten seconds later we followed, heading back down the hall to our rooms.

TL stopped at his. "It's ten o'clock. The opening meeting is in thirty minutes. I'll meet you in the lobby."

Beaker and I nodded, continuing on. We passed room after room, some with blaring loud TVs, others quiet. We got to ours and slipped the card key in the lock. No sounds muffled through the cracks. Maybe the twins had left.

"Hi!" Jessy and Lessy perked up when we opened our door.

Or maybe not.

"Hi." I noted the lack of enthusiasm in my return.

Beaker disappeared into the bathroom.

"So where ya'll from?!"

Vaguely, I registered the question as I glanced to the ceiling. *Eduardo Villanueva is up there right now.*

Slowly, I pulled my focus down to the bed closest to the wall—the same bed the twins currently sat on, propped against the headboard. I narrowed in on the shark behind their backs. What if one of them accidentally pressed the fin?

Both twins turned and looked at the shark, and I snapped to attention.

"Sorry." I laughed. "Brain fade."

They turned back around, and I plopped down on the other bed, recalling their last question. "Tiffany and I are from California. How about you two?"

"Giiive us an A!" They steepled their skinny arms above their heads. "Alabama!"

I grinned, while my mind hyperdrived. I wanted to get them

out of here so I could get inside that bed. I wanted to look at the equipment and get set up. I wanted to tap into Eduardo's room.

Actually, I needed to get the twins off that bed permanently in case one of them pressed the fin.

Beaker came from the bathroom, pressing her fingertips to her forehead. "Can you all do something for me?"

The twins nodded. "Sure!"

"Can you please not talk in so many Ex! Cla! Ma! Tion! Points?!" Beaker slid her hands down her face. "You're giving me a headache."

I closed my eyes on a silent groan. *Beeeaaaker.*

"For real?" one twin asked, and I snapped open my eyes.

Beaker sat down in the desk chair. "For real."

The twins looked at each other, and, gradually, matching smiles lit their faces. Real, happy, genuine smiles. Not the fake ones they'd flashed before.

The twin on the left slid down on her pillow. "Oh, thank you."

Her voice sounded different now. Deeper. More relaxed.

"Yeah." The twin on the right toed her purple-and-white tennis shoes off. "We don't even want to be here."

Well, isn't this an interesting twist?

Twin on the left punched the pillow beneath her head. "Our momma makes us do all these stupid events. This is our twelfth year of competitive cheer."

"Your *twelfth* year?" Beaker asked. "How old are you?"

Twin on the right brought her outstretched legs up into a crossed position. "We're nineteen years old." She pointed between me and Beaker. "Thought we were twelve or something, didn't ya?"

Yeah, actually, I had.

"I know. I know." Twin on the left raised her hands in the air. "Why, you ask, are we nineteen and still letting our momma tell us what to do?" She dropped her arms over her eyes. "Weee dooon't knooowww."

Twin on the right patted her sister. "One more year. That's all we need. And then we'll have a record deal and our own money."

"Record deal?" I questioned.

"See." Twin on the right turned to us. "We're singers. Country music. Faith Hill's our favorite." She narrowed her eyes at me. "You kinda look like her, ya know?"

Twin on the left lifted her arms from her eyes. "No, she doesn't."

"Yes, she does." This came from the twin on the right.

Beaker and I looked at each other.

"Anyway," twin on the right continued, "any day now we'll have our record deal."

Asian, twin, country music singers. Interesting.

Twin on the left rolled over, propping her head in her hand. "Enough about us. What about you two?"

I shrugged. "Nothing special. Average ordinary girls. Ana and Tiffany, at your service." If they only knew.

Twin on the right pouted her bottom lip. "Bummer. I was

hoping you were spies or something. Then we could all be undercover together. Jessy and Lessy, the hidden country talent. Ana and Tiffany, out for cold blood."

Beaker and I gave our best, ha-ha-that's-so-funny-spies-snort-snort laugh.

"Since we're going to be together for the whole competition," I suggested, "I suppose we should be able to tell you apart." This twin-on-the-left, twin-on-the-right business was about to drive me nuts.

"Oh, sure. We get that all the time." They scrambled together, kneeling side by side on the bed.

"Look at our faces." Twin on the right lifted her left brow. "What do you see that's different?"

I studied one face, then the next, and back to the first. I glanced at Beaker. "Well?"

"Scar."

"That's what I got." I pointed to the twin on the right. "You've got a scar running through your left brow." A scar so slight I would have never noticed it if I hadn't really studied their faces.

Twin on the right bounced her scarred brow. "I'm Jessy. Jagged-scar Jessy."

Lessy bounced off the bed, rattling the headboard and drawing my attention to the shark.

I eyeballed the fin. I had to get them off that bed. "Do you, um, mind if we sleep in that bed instead of this one?"

Jessy wedged her foot back into one of her purple-and-white tennis shoes. "Why?"

Why? I hadn't expected her to ask why. "Because . . . because . . ." Because there's a secret panel in your bed.

"Because," Beaker stood, "Ana's got this thing about sleeping near windows. She's afraid the boogeyman's going to climb in and get her. She's got to be near the wall."

With my best, innocent face, I shrugged. "I'm a freak that way. You don't mind, do you?"

Jessy tightened her laces. "Nope. But if the boogeyman comes in the door, he'll get you first."

I laughed. "I'll take my chances."

Lessy checked herself in the mirror. "Let's go. We don't want to be late for the *opening ceremony*. Yeah!" She rolled her eyes.

Laughing at her mock enthusiasm, we filed out of the room and down the hall. Beaker pressed the elevator button, and we waited.

Lessy and Jessy began discussing lyrics to a song they were working on, and, slowly, the discussion turned into an argument. Then Lessy started singing to block out her sister, and I had to admit she had a pretty darn good voice.

The elevator door slid open. Four men stood against the back wall—three overly muscular and one average, ranging in height from five eight to six one. Dressed in black suits, with dark hair and tanned skin, their faces displayed no expression as they stared at us.

Realizing who these men were, my stomach dropped. I was about to get in the elevator with them. I took a silent, deep breath and ran my gaze over each of their faces. Scrutinizing their features, I stopped at the last one on the right. The average-built one, but the tallest. The only one with silver glinting in his dark hair.

Eduardo Villanueva. My parents' killer.

My jaw tightened as I took in his tight curly hair, sinister brown eyes, and dark shadowed cheeks.

Lessy and Jessy stepped onto the elevator, still arguing and singing, oblivious to the four men.

Beaker turned, purposefully bumping into me, silently telling me to snap out of it.

I forced myself to drag my focus away from Eduardo's awful face when all I wanted to do was fly into the elevator and gouge out his emotionless eyes. I wanted to scream at him for what he'd done to my parents, to my life.

Instead, I sniffed, cleared my throat, and then lightly coughed. *Cover for me.* "Oh, I forgot something in the room. I'll meet you guys down there."

Lessy and Jessy didn't even hear me. Beaker nodded. She'd gotten my code.

I flicked one last look to Eduardo before turning from the elevator. With his head bent toward the man beside him, he listened to whatever the man was whispering. Probably discussing what horrible thing they planned to do next.

The elevator door slid closed. I hurried back down the hall and into our room, locked the door, and ran over to the bed.

I studied the body of the wooden shark and the fin attached to the top. I didn't see how anything could serve as a release button.

I leaned over the pillows and pushed the fin.

Nothing.

I pushed again, harder.

Nothing.

Crawling onto the bed, I traced my fingers around the edge of the fin. A slight gap existed where it had been attached to the headboard. A gap so tiny, no one would even notice it unless they felt for it.

I balled up my hand and knocked it hard, once, quick, with the side of my fist. It rattled the headboard.

Click. The bed shifted a little.

Scrambling off the bed, I surveyed it from head to foot and back up again. Nothing appeared different.

I yanked off the pillows and covers and threw them onto the other bed. Lifting up the mattress, I peered beneath.

Nothing but a thin piece of plywood.

Huh.

I got down on my hands and knees and looked underneath the bed. Carpet, hair, dust, a suspicious stain, and one forgotten flip-flop. Nothing else.

With a sigh, I sat up and glanced over to the clock. I'd already been up here ten minutes. I needed to hurry up and figure this out and get down to the meeting.

Okay, think, GiGi, think. You've got 191 IQ points. Put them to work. One bed with a hidden panel, one without. I knew I released the panel because I'd heard the click. And the bed shifted. So I had the correct bed. I hadn't misunderstood Nalani.

I glanced from the unmade, secret panel bed to the other one, and it hit me. Compare one with the other.

I lifted the mattress of the made bed and peeked underneath.

Bingo!

There was no plywood, just regular strips of wood supported its mattress.

Turning back to my bed, I wedged my fingers under the plywood and lifted to reveal a hidden compartment. Four trays set side by side as large as the king-size bed.

Audio and visual monitoring. TCVC cables, Socarmi recorders, Lome cameras, Wako lenses, Nociv monitors, and on and on and on.

Sweet. Top of the line. Every single thing from the equipment list.

Metal arms supported the plywood on both sides and held up the mattress. Locking the arms in the up position, I picked up a TCVC cable right as my phone vibrated. Yanking it from my pocket, I checked the encrypted display. Punching in my password, I decoded the message from TL.

TAKING ROLL. DOWN HERE. NOW.

I released the lock on the arms and brought the plywood back down. I banged the side of my fist into the fin and heard the click. I tried to lift the plywood just to make sure it was locked back in place. Sure enough, it didn't budge.

Quickly, I spread all the covers and pillows back in place and then hurried from the room.

I zipped down the hall, cut through the ice machine alcove, then the stairs, and raced across the lobby. I caught Nalani's eye with a where-do-I-go face. She discreetly pointed to a closed conference room door.

Quietly, I clicked it open and slipped inside. The coaches lined the back wall, and the cheer competitors sat in blue plastic chairs, filling the large room. The current America's Cheer team stood across the front dressed in matching red-white-and-blue shorts and T-shirts.

The one with the microphone pointed to someone in the crowd. She didn't look happy. "Get up."

Every head in the room silently turned in that direction.

I searched the crowd, curious what was going on.

"You." The microphone woman jabbed her finger. "In the red-and-white ribbon. Get up."

Red-and-white ribbon? Oh, no.

"Now," microphone lady echoed.

From the crowd, a dark-haired girl slowly stood.

Beaker.

9

Narrowing her eyes, the America's Cheer team leader pointed across the crowd to Beaker. "Spit it out."

Beaker lifted her brows, all innocent. "Spit what out?"

The team leader buried her lips in the microphone. "The gum."

Throughout the crowd, cheerleaders gasped.

I rolled my eyes.

Beaker delicately cleared her throat. "I don't have any gum."

Team leader crooked her finger. "Come here."

Beaker inched her way past the other cheerleaders sitting in her row and out into the aisle. Whispers trickled through the crowd as she walked down to the front. In unison, the current America's Cheer team authoritatively shook their heads at her.

This was ridiculous.

The team leader pinched Beaker's chin. "Open up."

Beaker did.

Pursing her lips, the team leader inspected Beaker's mouth. "Tongue."

She lifted her tongue.

Letting go of Beaker's chin, the team leader turned toward the crowd. "Who in here saw this competitor with gum?"

Almost everyone's hand went up.

Come on, people.

The team leader turned back to Beaker. "Clearly, you have swallowed it. Give me three times around the room. The cheer is 'G-U-M. Gum makes me look like a bum.'" The team leader leaned in. "And make it look good, or you're going to do it again."

Beaker's jaw clenched, and I could almost visualize the steam shooting from her ears.

I glanced down the row of people with me along the back wall. Stoically, TL stood near the end, keeping his gaze glued on Beaker.

His concentrated expression reminded me of the Rissala mission. He'd taught me how to send supportive, mental energy to Wirenut.

I know. It sounds weird. But it really works.

I turned my attention back to Beaker at the front and focused all my brain cells on sending her you-can-do-this vibes.

Inch by inch her cheeks crept upward into a gigantic, face-splitting grin. She took off around the room, clapping and jogging. "G-U-M! Gum makes me look like a bum!"

She circled around the back, came right past me, and didn't even spare me a glance.

I bet she hated me right now. Thanks to me and my friendly gum, she was running laps.

Beaker went down the room's other side and back across the front. "G-U-M! Gum makes me look like a bum!"

Some of the girls sarcastically clapped with her; others snickered. A few started bee-bopping in their chairs.

How would they feel if they were the ones put on the spot? I bet they wouldn't find it so entertaining then.

Beaker circled three complete times, smiling as she jogged, clapped, and chanted. She didn't look at me once.

She trotted to a stop back at the front and went straight into a back handspring. She came out of it and into a liberty, with her right foot on the inside of her left knee and her arms straight up. "Go, America's Cheer!"

And make it look good, or you're going to do it again.

Beaker's handspring definitely made it look good.

The America's Cheer team did matching liberties. "Go, America's Cheer!"

Everyone in the crowd hopped to their feet. "Go, America's Cheer!"

And then the place broke into wild applause. They were like possessed, brain-washed cheerleaders.

You will *be obnoxiously excited. You* will *snicker and make fun of others. You* will *spell everything you say.*

I smiled. Sometimes I really amused myself.

The cheering died down, and everyone took their seats again.

The team leader brought the microphone back to her mouth. "Okay. Let's finish taking roll, then we'll briefly go over the schedule and break for lunch."

Quickly, she went through the list, hitting my name a fourth of the way down and Beaker's a little after.

After she finished, the team leader shuffled some papers. "Each of you has a schedule in your registration packets. That schedule could change, depending on various things. You will be notified immediately of any changes. You are expected to be prompt for meals. Breakfast at seven, lunch at noon, dinner at five. All mornings are reserved for physical fitness and learning new routines. Afternoons are for run-throughs, team practice, and meetings. Evenings will be group functions. All contestants are expected to attend everything. Any absences mean points deducted from your team's final score."

On and on she went, seeming to fill every minute of every day. I didn't know how we would find time to do the things we needed to do for our mission.

"Dismissed," the team leader announced without asking for questions.

Girls filed passed me as I hung back, waiting for Beaker and TL.

"I'll have some juice, but that's it. I weighed in two pounds too heavy this morning."

"This bra is driving me nuts."

"Oh my *God*! My ribbon broke!"

"Good thing nobody saw the gum in *my* mouth."

"Hi!" Jessy and Lessy waved as they passed me.

I waved back.

With Beaker behind him, TL grabbed my arm and kept right

on going out the door. We cut off from the lunch line, down a hallway, and around a corner.

He glanced around to make sure we were alone and let go of my arm. He did not look happy. Pulling the blue pyramid from his pocket, he rotated it on. "Where were you?"

"I-I was in my room looking at the equipment."

"You are always, *always* to inform me of where you are and what you are doing." His jaw hardened. "Do we understand each other?"

"Y-yes, sir." But I thought this was *my* mission. I thought *I* was the one leading.

"You designed this mission," he continued, "but it doesn't mean you act on your own accord. I am the one who is ultimately in charge. I have to know where you are at all times. What if something had happened? What if something had gone wrong? What if someone from home base had contacted me and wanted to know your whereabouts? I can't say 'I don't know.' How do you think that would make me look? Us look?"

I hadn't thought about it like that. I swallowed. "I'm sorry. I should've texted you to let you know I was going back to the room."

TL took a step back. "I'm not saying you can't make your own decisions. I'm saying you *must* keep me informed of your locale."

TL turned to Beaker. "Or *you* should've told me. We're a team. We work as a unit."

Beaker and I nodded.

"Okay. Enough said." His cell phone buzzed, and, unclipping it from his waistband, he checked the display and answered his phone, "One second." He reached inside his pocket and pulled out two sugar packets. "It's the crystallized siumcy Beaker created. Nalani slipped me a couple packs. Make sure each of your roommates ingests this. The Tricsurv it goes with is in your equipment supplies. You'll know where your roommates are at all times."

Beaker turned to me. "What's a Tricsurv?"

I took a second to simplify the explanation in my brain. "The Tricsurv is a tracker. It looks like a computer chip and is usually inserted into a specialized watch. But since we're not allowed to wear watches, Chapling and I rigged everyone's cell phone to accept it. It'll give us our roommates coordinates at all times."

"When did you create that?" Beaker asked.

I shook my head. "I didn't. The Specialists already had it. When you told David and me about your powdered GPS compound, I knew it would work perfect with the Tricsurv. Tricsurv's been used for years in GPS situations. By the way, does the siumcy taste like anything?"

"Nothing," Beaker answered. "The twins won't even know."

I pocketed the sugar packets, excited to use them.

"Okay. I don't want either of you skipping meals on this trip. Keep your energy up." TL strode off down the hall, and we headed back the way we came.

"Let me give David a quick update." I got out my cell and punched UNEXPECTED ROOMATES. LOCATED EQUIPMENT . . . SAW EDUARDO.

He responded within seconds. FOCUS ON DNA DUST NEXT . . . YOU OKAY?

I knew he was referring to the "saw Eduardo" part. I WILL BE. BYE.

BYE.

Beaker untied the ribbon from around her neck and crammed it in her pocket. "This thing's choking me."

"Sorry about the gum," I apologized.

She shrugged. "Whatever."

"That back handspring was pretty impressive."

She smiled a little.

We crossed through the hotel's lobby and walked into the large meeting area that would serve as America's Cheer's meal room for the week.

A buffet stretched along the side wall. Tables and chairs had been set up cafeteria style, already occupied by bubbly cheerleaders eating their food.

Lessy and Jessy sat right in the center. They waved to us. "We saved you seats," they yelled over the chattering noise.

We waved back.

The buffet line had died down to nothing. We grabbed plates and loaded up. Turkey sandwiches, potato salad, chips, apple wedges, ginger cookies, carrots with ranch dressing, and cheese cubes.

I took some of everything and extras of the cookies. I didn't realize how *hungry* I was.

Beaker and I wove around the tables, heading toward Lessy and Jessy. Whispers followed us.

"What cows."

"Oh my God. Did you see all their food?"

"And they think they're going to make the team?" Snort. "Not on that diet."

I glanced around at the other girls' plates. Carrot sticks on one. A piece of turkey on another. One lousy scoop of potato salad on another.

No wonder they were all so skinny.

Beside me, Beaker grabbed a cookie and shoved it in her mouth. "Mmm-mmm, good."

I rolled my lips in so I wouldn't laugh.

We sat our plates down at Lessy and Jessy's table.

"Hi!" I greeted them cheerily, then realized I didn't need to. This was Lessy and Jessy, aspiring country singers. They were acting a role just like us.

In fact—I glanced around—I'd bet there were more people who didn't want to be here either.

"Lord." Jessy blinked a few times. "You're really going to eat all that?"

"Yep, and I'll probably go back for seconds," I bragged.

Lessy put her hand over her heart. "My hero."

"Dangit." I got back up. "I forgot to get sweet tea. Ya'll want some?"

They looked unexcitedly at their water, then across the room to the drinks table.

"Oh, come on," I teased. "Live a little. I dare you to have *extra* sugar in it." Nobody could refuse a dare.

They both narrowed their eyes. "Bring it on."

I put my hand over my heart. "My heroes."

They giggled.

Beaker and I crossed the room to the drinks table. She grabbed two teas and I did, too, dumping in real sugar combined with my tracking "sugar."

"That was almost *too* easy," Beaker mumbled as we made our way back to Lessy and Jessy.

Eagerly, they gulped down half of their tea. Jeez, these girls needed to live a little.

Jessy wiped her mouth. "Nice gum chanting, Tiffany."

Beaker playfully smirked.

The pink-and-green team out of Portland strolled past, slanting us a haughty look. What the heck? They'd been so friendly earlier.

Jessy leaned close to me. "Don't you hate that? To your face everyone's all smiley and friendly. But they're all a bunch of back stabbers. Especially if they think you're better than them."

Better than them? I almost snorted. I could barely do a back handspring.

"Don't look." Lessy surreptitiously pointed her carrot across the room. "But I heard the red-haired girl on the black-and-yellow team is a genius. She's got an IQ higher than like Einstein or something."

A genius? I turned and looked.

Jessy yanked me back around. "She said don't look."

"Sorry."

A genius? Wow. For some reason I hadn't thought of cheer-leaders as geniuses.

Lessy gulped down the rest of her tea. "We're going to walk down to the beach. Wanna come?"

I shook my head. "Nah. I'm going to watch some TV." Perfect time to check out the equipment and possibly rig Eduardo Villanueva's room for surveillance.

Beaker swallowed her turkey bite. "Me, too." She checked her watch. "There's only thirty minutes before our first practice."

Jessy grabbed all of her and Lessy's garbage. "Suit yourselves. Later, ya'll."

We waved as they strolled off, quickly shoved in a mouthful of food, and hightailed it out of there.

Up the elevator, down the hall, and into our room we went. Beaker texted TL to let him know where we were while I texted Nalani.

EV LOCATION? I typed.

ROOM. Nalani responded.

Perfect. "He's in his room. We can do the DNA dust."

Quickly, I showed Beaker how to open the bed's secret panel.

I took two Tricsurv chips and plugged them into my phone and into hers. A satellite image of our hotel and surrounding area flicked onto the display. Two red dots popped up.

"That'd be Lessy and Jessy." I tapped the dots. "And they're on the beach just like they said. The Tricsurv will beep when they get within twenty feet of us."

"That's barely enough time to put all this back together."

"I know." I put the phone on the nightstand. "We need to work quickly."

Beaker lifted a tray full of all sorts of powders, liquids, and chemistry stuff from the secret panel.

She grabbed a bag of clear crystals.

While she began mixing the DNA dust, I pulled the mini-laptop from my luggage, powered up, and connected to our satellite. I slipped on my glasses and keyed in the scrambler code and the coordinates to Eduardo Villanueva's room. The satellite zeroed in on the hotel and X-rayed through the roof and straight into the presidential suite.

Indeed, Eduardo was there along with all his men. And an easy chair sat right on top of where I needed to drill.

Good. No one would see a thing. "I'll use the silencer so they won't hear. It's a one-sixteenths bit for your syringe, right?"

"Yes."

From one of the hidden trays, I retrieved the drill, inserted a one-sixteenths bit, and screwed on the silencer.

I replaced my glasses with protective goggles and climbed onto our bed and over to the far edge, where it sat only a few inches from the room's corner. Standing on the edge, I silently drilled through the ceiling straight up into Eduardo's suite.

Plaster sprinkled me as I pulled the drill back out. "Ready?"

"Yeah." Beaker poured a fine red dust into a syringe and handed it to me. "Remember to go slow to give time for the dust to dissipate, turn invisible, and absorb into Eduardo and his men's skin."

Over the next few days, anywhere they went, we'd be able to see their DNA trailing behind them. Whatever they got into, we'd have proof.

I inserted the syringe into the hole and slowly admitted the dust. "Ya know," I whispered, "this DNA dust you created is incredibly brilliant."

Beaker shrugged. "Yeah, yeah. Whatever."

Whatever? There was no way I could've come up with something like this. But then, I was the computer specialist, not the chemist.

Finishing off with the dust, I handed Beaker the syringe and she gave me a tube of spackle.

I squeezed it into the hole, and the ceiling looked normal again. "Now all we gotta do is figure out how to track him electronically."

"Somehow I doubt we'll get close enough to put crystallized siumcy in his ice tea."

Suddenly, the Tricsurv in my cell phone beeped, and Beaker and I jolted into action.

We quickly tossed everything back in the trays, slammed the shark's fin, threw the covers and pillows back in place, cut the light, and jumped into bed.

Our door opened and in tiptoed Jessy and Lessy. Beneath the covers, my heart raced.

"You asleep?" One of them whispered. "Thought you said you were going to be watching TV."

Beaker yawned. "It's all right."

Lessy ripped open the curtains. "We met the *hottest* guy."

I squinted against the afternoon sunlight. "Yeah?"

Jessy jumped onto their king-size bed. "Oh, yeah. Major hot. His name's CJ, and he's eighteen."

Lessy hopped onto our bed. "Major hot. Major, major, *major* hot."

Scooting my legs out of the way, I laughed, trying to sound carefree, when all I could think was, *Oh my God, she's bouncing on our secret panel bed!*

Jessy dove between me and Beaker. "He's got blond hair and blue eyes, and did I tell you he's hot?"

I moved over, trying to protect the headboard.

Lessy body-slammed her sister, and, giggling, they rolled into me. I caught a quick glimpse of Beaker trying to come between the twins and the headboard a split second before one of them rammed into the fin release lever.

Click. The bed shifted.

They stilled. "What was that?"

someone rapped on our door.

"I'll get it." Silently thankful for the distraction, I leapt off the bed. I had no *clue* how to answer the twins' question.

I opened the door to see TL in the threshold.

"Ready for practice?" he asked.

"Sure."

We spent the entire rest of the day practicing cheers, doing routine run-throughs, and sitting in meetings. The next day was just the same, and when dinner finally came, I couldn't wait to eat and get back to our room. I just wished the twins would go to the beach or something so I could get some work done.

After dinner, my roommates and I filed into our room. The twins plopped across our bed. What was it with them and our bed?

As soon as we closed the door, someone knocked.

I opened it to an America's Cheer team member.

She flipped a paper over on her clipboard. "Hi! There's been a change in the schedule. The bonfire rally scheduled for tomorrow night will be tonight on the beach in thirty minutes."

Bonfire rally? The schedule said free time until tomorrow

morning. I'd had things planned. Lots of things. Like ditching the twins and setting up more surveillance. Figuring out how to physically plant a tracking device in addition to the DNA tracker on Eduardo. And possibly following him if he went somewhere.

Using a red-white-and-blue pen, the America's Cheer team member checked us off on her pad. "This is a mandatory event, so everyone must be present."

I planted the fakest, I'm-so-thrilled smile on my face. "Sounds super! I'll let my roommates know."

She two-finger waved me. "Too-da-loo. See you in thirty."

I waved back.

"This sucks," Lessy pouted when I closed the door.

"Yeah," Jessy joined her. "We were totally going to blow this joint and go into town for the night."

Beaker snorted. "And do what? Did you not see this place when you came in? There's nothing to do but exercise your neat and tidy skills."

Playfully, she shoved the twins off our bed and spread out on it. "And stay off my bed, would ya? I like my space. I don't play well with others."

Not bad, Beaker. Maybe that would keep them off our bed.

Lessy checked herself in the mirror. "I'm not going to sit around here for thirty minutes. I'm going to go on down." She turned to us. "Coming?"

"I need to use the bathroom," Beaker and I answered at the exact same time.

Jessy laughed. "Just don't do it together."

The twins bounded out the door. As soon as they left, I snatched up my cell phone from the nightstand and did a quick scan. Two red dots moved as they rode the elevator down.

I nodded to Beaker. "They're in the lobby."

I quickly texted David to let him know our progress. DNA DUST IN PLACE. TRACKERS ON ROOMMATES.

He responded right away. GOTCHA. GET ELECTRONIC TRACKER ON EDUARDO NOW.

Beaker hopped off our bed, lifted the mattress and plywood, and grabbed the rose-tinted, silver-framed glasses from one of the hidden trays, the same glasses she'd showed us in our pre-op meeting. "These are for the DNA dust. We'll be able to see anywhere Eduardo goes. It's all we've got until we figure out a way to put an electronic tracker on him."

I nodded. "Good. I'll let Nalani know to text us if he's on the move."

Beaker pulled out another one of the trays. "What do we have in the way of trackers?"

I hit send to text Nalani, then ran my gaze over everything in the trays. "Breath mints. Pepper. Stick-on freckles. Blow darts that simulate mosquito stings . . ." I snatched everything up, gave half to Beaker, and we loaded down our backpacks. "Let's take it all so we'll be ready in any situation. One way or another we're going to get a tracker on Eduardo."

Quickly, we put our bed back in order and headed from the room.

TL stood with Coach Luke at the elevator.

"Hi!" We joined them.

TL rubbed his hands together. "You girls ready for the bonfire?"

We enthusiastically nodded.

Coach Luke tapped the DNA glasses propped on my head. "Those sure are spiffy glasses."

"Thanks!" Who actually used the word *spiffy*? And by God, if he put a fingerprint on the lenses . . .

The elevator dinged, and as the doors slid open, four men in black suits came into view. I caught my breath. Eduardo stood in the back with his guys, in the exact same position they had been in earlier today. Their blank expressions dropped ever so slightly with annoyance at seeing us. I bet they *were* tired of us bubbly cheerleaders. And this was only the beginning.

Just then, my phone vibrated. I knew it was Nalani texting me back that Eduardo was on the move.

Okay, focus. Here's a chance to get a tracker on him. My eyes narrowed with orneriness. Maybe I should make it a little more annoying for them. I *am* a cheerleader, after all.

Yeah, why not?

As I bounded inside, I quickly rummaged in my backpack and pulled out the first small electronic tracker—the tracking bug—that I could get a grip on. "Hi!" I said cheerily, my ponytail boinging behind me. "Are you all with America's Cheer?"

Eduardo and his men made no move. They didn't even look at me.

Keeping my grin, I blinked a few times. "Are you all with America's Cheer?"

Slowly, all four sets of dark eyes moved over to me. Simultaneously, they shook their heads.

Still grinning, I blinked. "Oh! Are you with the hotel?"

They shook their heads.

Grin. Blink. "Oh! Are you here for vacation or business?"

They shook their heads.

I reached out and tugged on the suit jacket of the man beside Eduardo. "You look *spiffy* enough to be here for some business meeting."

"Miss."

Maintaining my grin, I turned to Eduardo. It was the first time I'd ever heard his deep voice. It caught me a little off guard, and I felt my stomach drop. I immediately thought of my parents and wondered if they had hated his voice as much as I did at this moment. "Yes?"

His lids fell slightly, hooding his menacing eyes. "Stop talking to us. And don't ever touch me or anyone with me again."

My grin faded as I nodded and forced myself to turn around. I wanted to ram my foot into his kneecap.

Beside me, Beaker cleared her throat. "I didn't get a chance to brush my teeth after dinner. Do you have those mints with you?"

I reached inside my backpack, pulled out the box of tracking mints, and handed them to her.

She opened the top, tapped one out, and tossed it into her mouth. "Mmm-mmm, good." She turned to Eduardo. "Want one?"

I laughed. I couldn't help myself.

The elevator dinged open, and we filed out.

TL waved on Coach Luke. "I'll be there in a sec. I want to talk to my girls."

Eduardo and his men filed past us, through the lobby with a dozen or so loudly gossiping cheerleaders, and straight out the door. I pulled the DNA detector glasses off my head and slipped them on. Sure enough, a red trail followed in their wake.

I lifted the glasses and checked out the difference. No trail existed. These things were cool.

Putting an arm around both of us, TL hugged us to his sides and companionably strolled with us down the hallway. We cut a corner and walked straight into a small meeting room.

He closed the door behind us, pulled the blue pyramid from his pocket, and rotated the top. He turned to me. "You know you stepped beyond boundaries in the elevator. What was the number one thing David taught you when you were designing this mission?"

I took off the glasses and looped them in my T-shirt. "Not to let personal emotions muddle effective decision making."

"Well, guess what? You just let your emotions make you stupid. Because that was the most ignorant thing I've ever seen you do."

His harsh words didn't make me feel guilty *or* apologetic. They made me downright mad. "So."

TL got right up in my face. "Young lady, you watch your tone with me *and* show some respect. This is the second time you've messed up. This mission is beginning to lack focus. You need to get back on track."

I clamped my teeth together so I wouldn't say anything I'd regret. This mission did *not* lack focus.

He held his steely eyes level with mine for a few long seconds, letting me see *he* was the one in charge.

I didn't tell him I'd transferred a tracking bug when I touched that man's suit. Being mad made me keep that information to myself. I'd track the guy myself and then go to TL with the information. He'd be proud of me then.

TL took a step back. "Beaker, give me a rundown."

She did, detailing everything we'd done on the mission so far. The whole time she talked, I stood beside her *itching* to get out of here and activate the tracking software on my cell phone. Eduardo and his men could be miles from here by now.

And the tracking bug I'd transferred to Eduardo's man could, at any time, be uncovered by a detector, if they had one. Then they would definitely know someone was here following them. So maybe transferring that bug hadn't been such a good idea.

Although, it was only a thirty-minute bug. It would dry up and fall off his jacket when that time had passed. And the DNA dust would only show where they'd been, not where they were going.

That was why I *had* to get a tracker into their bloodstream via the mints, or the sugar, or the simulated mosquito sting. Trackers in the blood were the only type that couldn't be detected and would definitely give us their coordinates.

"GiGi?"

I snapped to attention. "What?" I glanced around. TL had gone on ahead to the bonfire.

"I said, are you ready?"

I grabbed Beaker's arm. "Listen, you gotta cover for me. I transferred a thirty-minute bug to one of Eduardo's men. If I don't go now and follow them, I'll lose them"

"What am I supposed to say if someone asks where you are?"

"I'm in the bathroom with girl issues," I said, taking out my cell phone and activating the tracking software. "No one argues when someone has girl issues."

Two red dots popped up on my screen. The twins. And a blue dot. Eduardo's man. I raced for the door. "Be back before you know it."

With a glance down the hall toward the lobby, I headed in the opposite direction, past a few rooms, and out the side exit door. I trailed along the length of the hotel to the front and slipped the rose-colored glasses back on.

I checked out the portico where two bellmen lingered near their stand, reviewing a logbook. A red DNA trail led from the hotel's front doors across the portico, and then stopped where Eduardo and his men must have gotten into a car. This was why we definitely needed a tracker on them. Anytime they got in a car, we'd lose their DNA trail.

Looking again at my cell phone, I confirmed the blue dot was still there. I took off down the long driveway, staying behind the bushes and palms, praying no one would see my tall blond self or red-and-white cheerleading getup. I wasn't exactly dressed for espionage.

In the distance, cheerleaders hooted and hollered at the bon-fire rally. Poor Beaker. At least she had Lessy and Jessy.

Streetlights kicked on along the hotel's driveway and down in town. To the right, the sun dipped into the ocean's horizon.

Perfect. It would be pitch-black in no time.

I reached the bottom of the driveway and checked the blue dot on my phone screen. Eduardo and his men had already made it across the five-mile wide island to the other side.

Shoving my phone into my warm-ups pocket, I snapped the flap and took off running through town.

I tried to make it look more like a healthy jog than a frantic chase. I didn't need anyone calling 911.

Hello, officer? There's this tall blond girl running for her life through town.

Wouldn't *that* be great?

I had said it before, but I would say it again. Thank God for PT back at the ranch. There was no *way* I could make this run without it.

One mile in, I passed a boy on a bike and cut a U-ie. "Hey, kid, let me borrow your bike. I'll give you twenty bucks."

The kid narrowed his eyes. "Let me see the money."

Smart kid. I reached into my back pocket and pulled out my zipper pouch, hoping I did indeed have twenty bucks.

Thirty in all. Phew. I gave him twenty and pointed to the

grocery store across the road. "I'll leave it in the bike rack in front of that store on the right. Cool with you?"

"Cool." He pocketed the money.

I climbed on his mini–dirt bike and away I went, pumping down the sidewalk, my knees nearly hitting my chest.

Twenty minutes later, I made it to the other side of the island. I stopped and checked my cell phone. The blue dot was beginning to fade, indicating the thirty-minute tracker was dissolving, but from what I could tell, Eduardo was to my right.

I rode into a deserted parking lot of the state park. Behind me stretched a half mile of beach highway leading back into town. In front of me spanned the dark ocean lit only by the half moon. To the left stood a small concrete visitor's station.

With the DNA glasses still on, I scanned the area. A red trail led from the parking lot, where the car must have dropped him and drove off, and onto the beach.

Leaving the bike, I followed the red trail across the beach and down the length of a long pier. The red trail stopped at the end of the pier, where a boat had probably picked him up.

There was no telling how far out he'd gone.

I unsnapped my pocket and pulled out the cell phone. I activated the audio recording/eavesdropping software Chapling had coded in.

Here went nothing.

I programmed it to record everything within a mile in front of me. Slowly, I scanned the ocean, moving from left to right, degree by degree, listening closely.

Static. Birds. Wind. Bugs. Nothing else.

I reprogrammed it for two miles and started over, left to right, degree by degree.

Bingo!

A faint conversation in what sounded like Spanish. Definitely Eduardo's deep, ugly voice.

Holding the phone steady, I pressed the record button and listened for fifteen solid minutes, wishing Parrot was here with me to translate immediately.

Through the phone I heard the boat's motor crank. Depressing the record button again, I sprinted back down the pier across the beach to the bike.

Down the highway, headlights pierced the night.

Crap.

Praying, *praying,* no one would see my blond head and flashy cheerleading outfit, I picked up the bike and ran for the visitor's station.

Right as the car pulled into the lot, I ducked into the shadows behind the concrete structure.

I drew in deep breaths and blew them out slowly, repeating the process a couple of times. Gradually, my thumping heart and heavy breaths normalized.

Peeking around the building's corner, I watched as a black Cadillac with tinted windows rolled to a stop.

A dark-haired man dressed in a suit climbed from the driver's side. I recognized him as one of the guys who had been in the elevator with Eduardo back at the hotel. I switched my phone to infrared mode, killed the flash, and snapped a picture of him.

He shut his door and leaned up against the car.

Minutes later, Eduardo and two more men emerged from the beach's darkness. I zoomed in on each face and got a picture.

They began speaking. From the distance between us their voices came across muffled, but I could still make out the conversation.

"What are we going to do with him?" one of the men asked in perfect English.

"Kill him," Eduardo responded, as if he was answering a pleasant question.

"And the woman and children?" the man asked.

"Did any of them see you deliver the money?"

The man nodded. "Two of them did."

Eduardo shrugged. "Kill them, too."

"How do you want it done?"

Eduardo stepped toward the car. "The usual—bullets to the head. All of them."

My whole body froze as I listened to them discuss killing an entire family. That easy. Bullets to the head. Just like my parents.

You can't just kill a whole family, I wanted to scream. What had they done that was so wrong?

The driver opened the door for Eduardo, the other men climbed in, and the car drove away.

I made myself get up when all I wanted to do was stay cowered in the shadows, grieving for the family that was about to die. A family that, although I didn't know them, was just like mine.

Crossing behind the visitor's center, I got a picture of the license plate as they pulled from the lot.

Waiting until its rear lights disappeared, I climbed on the bike and pedaled my way back down the highway, through town, and to the grocery store with the bike rack. I walked the remaining mile to the hotel, my footsteps heavy to match my thoughts.

David had said not to let my emotions cloud the mission. But this time I couldn't help it. I thought about what my life would have been like if Eduardo hadn't ruined it. Hadn't taken the two most important things from me. Where would I be right now? Still in Iowa? I'd probably live in a really cool house with maybe a dog. We'd go on family vacations every year. I'd help my mom cook dinner at night and help my dad on the weekends do lawn work. My mom and I might have planted a flower garden. Our Christmas tree would have been medium-size, with white lights and blue decorations.

Someone pushed through the exit door of the hotel as I approached, bringing me from my reverie. I walked in the hotel and took the stairs up to our floor.

Sweaty from my bike ride and worn out from my thoughts, I entered our room. There sat TL and Beaker. Him on one bed, her on the other, and the blue pyramid on the nightstand between them.

I knew I was in trouble. It didn't take a genius to figure that out.

TL indicated the desk chair. "Sit."

I glanced at Beaker as I sat. She gave me a good-luck look. "Where're the twins?"

"Downstairs," Beaker answered, "practicing their routine for tomorrow."

Nodding, I turned my attention to TL, wanting to get the whole thing over with.

"Back at the ranch I told you that you were developing into a person I hadn't expected you to. At least, not this quickly." He shifted on the bed. "There's nothing wrong with being an independent thinker and making your own decisions. But there's a time and place for that sort of thing. This isn't it. There's something wrong when you're with a team and you're not using them."

He pointed across the room to me. "You are sixteen and a half. Letting you plan this mission was a test. You have not had enough training to be making some of the decisions you're making, like going after Eduardo by yourself. And you have enough intelligence in that head of yours to understand that."

Reluctantly, my brain agreed with him.

"GiGi, you are extremely gifted. In so many ways. I don't think you fully comprehend what you are capable of." TL shook his head. "But I'm really disappointed in you. And that's something I never thought I'd say to you."

I glanced down at the carpeting, my heart sinking, but all I could think about was the family. "There's a family that's about to die," I whispered.

"I know. I know where you've been. I know what you've done. And I know you have a recording and pictures."

"WHAT?" I brought my eyes up to his.

"I told you I'd always be watching you."

TL reached inside his pocket and pulled out a cell phone. "Everything you did tonight is right here." TL held the phone up. "Courtesy of Chapling."

I sat up in the desk chair. "How?"

"I had monitoring devices installed everywhere. Your phone. The stitching in your clothes." He waved his hand around. "This hotel room."

Anger bubbled inside of me.

"You are sixteen and a half," TL reminded me again. "And this is the first mission you've designed. Of course I'm going to monitor you. If you would put aside your agitation, logic would point that out."

"But don't you trust me?"

His brows lifted. "What have you done here in Barracuda Key to earn my trust?"

That question bounced around in my head for a few seconds, and I came up with . . . nothing. And if I had done something, it was negated by the other. I'd purposefully deceived him.

I sighed.

"I see logic is trickling in." TL stood. "From this moment, this mission is officially mine. You do not say or do anything unless it's a direct order from me. And one more anything out of you and I'm sending you back to California. Beaker and I can finish this on our own."

"What about the family?"

"I'll do everything in my power to help them, but odds are we're not going to find out who they are. I'm sorry. Get the recording sent back to home base so Parrot can translate it." Grabbing the blue audio-blocker pyramid, he strode straight past me and out the door.

Beaker took in a breath like she wanted to say something, but I ignored her. I walked over and turned on my laptop, connected my phone, and punched in the scrambler code.

HI. Chapling typed.

HI. I typed back. Usually his online presence made me smile. Not this time, though. I really wasn't in the mood.

WHATCHA GOT FOR ME?

NEED PARROT TO TRANSLATE. I clicked some keys. SENDING NOW.

I watched as my screen flicked, transmitting the recording back to home base.

GOT IT, he typed. YOU OKAY, SMARTGIRL?

Amazing how he could pick up on my mood from across cyber space.

I'M FINE, I typed back. I didn't need him worried about me.

My cell phone beeped. I checked the display. "Lessy and Jessy are coming."

GOTTA GO, I quickly told Chapling.

BYE! BE SAFE.

I closed my laptop, and Beaker and I lapsed into silence, staring off into space, waiting for the twins to appear. All I could think of was how bad I'd screwed up and of the family that was going to die.

Blowing out a silent breath, I dropped my head into my hand.

"Um . . ." Beaker started.

"It's okay. You don't have to say anything."

"I'm sorry you know people are about to die."

I barely nodded. Sometimes this new life of mine really sucked. I didn't like having the inside information on bad stuff that was about to happen, especially when I was powerless to do anything.

My cell phone buzzed, and I punched in the password to decode the incoming message.

THINKING OF YOU.

I silently read the message from David and smiled inwardly at the comfort and peace it brought. I didn't tell him how I'd screwed up.

ME TOO, I typed back.

▦ ▦ ▦

THE NEXT DAY CAME WAY too early and was way too packed. Breakfast, training, rehearsal, lunch, and break. More training, another rehearsal, dinner, then a team-building activity where we all sat around with linked arms, singing. And in between, in the few moments we got to ourselves, I had to switch gears and try to focus on the mission.

At the end of the day, Beaker and I trudged into our room after the annoying sing-along.

Frustrated, I plopped down into the desk chair. "We haven't done *anything* today regarding the real reason we're here."

"Tell me about it," Beaker grumbled. "I can't believe I'm about to say this, but I'm happy Coach Capri made me work as hard as she did. There's no way I would've been prepared for all this cheery stuff without all her barking." Beaker jabbed her finger in my direction. "But tell her I said any of that, and you're dead."

I laughed.

Our door clicked open, and Lessy and Jessy bounded in. "Hi!"

"Hi," Beaker and I returned.

Jessy flopped across their bed. "Looord, I hate cheer training."

Smiling at her whining, I slipped out of my chair and onto the floor, where my backpack sat under the desk. I unzipped it and dug around, searching for a lollipop.

On the bed, Beaker stretched out on her stomach. "Me, too."

Lessy plunked down next to her sister. "You've got the hottest coach."

Jessy grabbed a pillow. "Yeah, everybody's talking about it."

Beaker and I glanced at each other. Yeah, TL *was* hot. Actually, the first time I saw him I thought he was the best-looking guy I'd ever seen.

"Ooh!" Jessy threw her hands up. "Speaking of hot. You know CJ, that blond guy we met yesterday?" She cut Beaker a sideways glance. "Guess who I saw talking to him?"

Beaker diverted her attention to the bedspread and suddenly became very interested in the pattern.

I found a pineapple lollipop in my backpack and unwrapped it. "Who?"

"Apparently he's a delivery guy for the hotel. He was in the lobby after lunch, and I saw him talking to our own little Tiffany." Lessy pursed her lips as she surveyed Beaker.

I slipped the lollipop in my mouth. "Is that so?" I teased.

Beaker shot me a snarl. It cheered me up.

"He asked me if I was here with the cheerleading thing." Beaker rolled her eyes. "As if he couldn't figure that out by looking at my stupid getup." She rolled off her bed. "I need a soda. Anybody want one?"

Actually, a soda sounded good. "I'll go with you." I dug around in my backpack and fished out some money.

Jessy started undressing. "Get me diet orange."

Lessy flipped on the TV. "Me, too. You'll have to go to the lobby, though. The vending machines on the floors don't carry orange." She cringed. "Sorry."

I shrugged. "No big deal."

Beaker and I left the room and got halfway to the elevator.

"Just a sec." I jogged back down the hall to TL's room and knocked.

Seconds passed, and, just as I turned to leave, he cracked open the door. He didn't look happy. Behind him, Nalani sat on a bed, wiping her cheeks.

I looked at TL. "Is everything okay?"

He moved in front of me, blocking my view of her. "What do you need?"

"Where's Coach Luke?"

"He went into town. What do you need?"

Obviously, TL and Nalani were having a personal issue, and he didn't want me asking about it. And frankly, it was none of my business. But . . . what was *wrong* with them?

TL lifted his brows.

"Sorry." I pointed down the hall to where Beaker stood. "We're going to go get some sodas. Just wanted to see if you wanted anything."

"I'm fine."

With a nod, I turned.

"Ana?"

I turned back.

"Thank you for asking."

I smiled a little. "You're welcome."

TL shut the door, and I trotted back to Beaker. We rode the elevator and headed down the long hall toward the back of the hotel where the vending machines were.

Beaker pushed open the door that led into the vending area and came to an abrupt stop. A blond guy stood at the snack machine, eyeing the selections. He had sun-dried, straight hair to his shoulders and was dressed in board shorts, a T-shirt, and flip flops. 'Surfer dude' popped into my mind first.

He looked up, and surprise lit his blue eyes. "Hey."

Beaker didn't respond, and so I answered back. "Hey."

He stepped forward and extended his hand. "I'm CJ." He nodded to Beaker. "I met Tiffany earlier today."

I stepped into the small room and shook his hand. "Ana."

CJ stood shorter than me, but definitely taller than Beaker. I'd say five feet eight. One side of his mouth lifted in a half smile, and instantly I recognized what the twins saw in him.

He turned his attention to Beaker. "How's it going?"

With a little nod, she glanced away. How cute. Who would've thought she'd be so shy?

"Um . . ." He started and then stopped. "Um, I was just heading to a beach party. My friends are already there. You wanna come?"

Beaker blushed. *Actually* blushed. "No, thanks."

CJ's brow twitched, and I could tell he was really bummed she'd turned him down. He cut his eyes to me. "You can come, too."

Poor guy. He was obviously hoping my agreement would persuade Beaker. "Thanks." I smiled to let him know I really meant it. "I'm tired. It's been a long day."

He shifted uncomfortably. "Well, okay then." He went back to the machine, quickly made his selection, and snatched up his chips. "See you all around."

"Nice to meet you," I said as he pushed through the door.

"You, too," he returned.

I moved over to the soda machine and fed in a dollar bill. "You could have gone with him if you wanted. You know that, right?"

Beaker shrugged.

I selected two diet orange drinks for the twins. "I mean, just because we're here on other business," I whispered in case anyone might be listening, "doesn't mean you can't go out."

She shrugged.

I fed another dollar in. "How do you think Wirenut met Cat?"

She shrugged.

I selected a regular cola for me. "Which do you want?"

She shrugged.

Sighing, I pressed regular for her, too. "You want to tell me what's going on?"

"Nothing," she grumbled. "I'm just not used to this, that's all."

"Used to what?"

Beaker flung her hand in the air. *"This."*

"This what?"

"Never mind." She reached past me, grabbed two of the drinks from the vending machine, and tucked them in her jacket pockets. "You wouldn't understand."

"Understand what?" Honestly, I had no idea what she was talking about.

Beaker shoved through the door and strode off.

Grabbing the two remaining drinks, I followed after her. "What's wrong with you?"

She shouldered open an exit door that led out near the hotel pool area and beach. "Just leave me alone. Go be . . . perfect or gorgeous or something."

Her gruff words didn't match her hunched shoulders. She needed some serious lightening up.

"Perfect? Are you serious?" I laughed, stepping through the exit door and into the night. "Did you just meet me? Come on. I trip over my own feet. I drop food on my clothes. I stumble over my words. I can barely carry on a conversation unless it deals with binary numbers and algorithms. And, oh yeah, I'm a social reject."

She marched off down a mulched path that led to the beach. "Whatever. You have the perfect looks and the perfect boyfriend. And no one's ever made fun of you."

"Oh, please. That's all anyone ever did back in Iowa. Everyone in the dorms thought I was weird." I glanced around the dimly lit path, assuring we were alone. "Being a Specialist is the first time I've ever felt somewhat normal."

Beaker turned around. "People thought you were weird?"

"How many girls do you know with a one-hundred-ninety-one IQ who spends her days buried in her own brain?"

"Just you."

"See?"

Beaker studied me for a couple of long seconds. "I guess we're both weird in our own weird way."

I smiled. "Seems like it."

Thoughtfully, she gazed through the night toward the beach.

I put my drinks down on a lounge chair and dried my hands on my shirt. "So are you going to tell me what's wrong?"

Beaker heaved a heavy sigh. "Don't laugh, okay?"

I held up my hands.

"I've never been on a date before. I've never had such a cute, normal guy like me. And I'm more than freaked about it because"—she motioned to her hair and clothes—"this isn't me."

I had the unnerving urge to hug her. Underneath all her gruffness, Beaker had a soft, sweet, insecure side. But I knew if I got gushy, touchy-feely, she'd push me away.

Instead, I shrugged. "I've never been on a date either."

She blinked. "David?"

I shook my head. "Nope. It's definitely on my list of things to do, though."

That earned a small laugh.

I took a step toward her. "Don't worry about CJ. And smile the next time you see him. It won't kill you." Listen to me giving relationship advice. "Something tells me he wouldn't care if you were Goth or not."

"Really?"

"Really. Come to think of it, I miss your Goth uniqueness. I don't like you looking like everyone else."

Beaker's lips twitched.

Playfully, I shoved her shoulder. "You're not so mean after all."

"Yeah, I am," she disagreed with a slight smile.

In that second it occurred to me her harshness was a wall to keep everyone at a distance. Put there because of the way she'd been treated over the years. In fact, I could've easily developed the same wall. Who would have thought Beaker and I were so emotionally similar?

I gave my head a quick shake, snapping out of my retrospective moment. Sometimes I could be quite the psychoanalyst.

My phone buzzed, and I checked the display. "It's David!"

Beaker snatched my drinks off the lounge chair and headed back up the path. "See ya back in the room."

"Okay." I pressed the Talk button on my phone.

"Hi," I greeted him with a huge grin, even though he couldn't see it.

"Hi, back."

His voice made my insides pure goosh.

"Where are you?" he asked.

I meandered down the path. "Heading toward the beach."

"What's at the beach? Another bonfire rally?"

"No. Beaker and I were having a private talk."

"Everything okay?"

"Yeah." I blew out a breath. "No. I mean, yeah, everything's okay with me and Beaker. But, no, not with me. Or, I don't know." All the mistakes I'd made on this mission came rushing at me, and I sighed in pure frustration. "David, I've really screwed up."

"What do you mean?"

"With you," I answered. "With this mission."

"Listen, as far as everything that happened back at the ranch between you and me? I don't want to think about it anymore. It's over with. We're fine. Can we do that? I know your emotions are running high over all this, and I understand that."

I made it to the beach and sat down in the sand. "My connection to this mission and my emotions are making me stupid."

"That's why I called. I know about everything that's happened. TL and I talk numerous times a day."

I stared up at the half moon. Great. Now I had to hear it from David, too. "And? Are you disappointed in me?"

"No. I wish I was there to hug you, though."

My heart paused. "Oh, David . . ." His quiet words sank deep into my soul, filling all the empty voids. I closed my eyes. "I needed to hear that so bad."

"GiGi, you should know TL's had me following you. I was right there watching you on that bike trailing Eduardo."

Silence. Long seconds ticked by as indignation hit me first, slowly followed by logical reasoning. Of course TL would have me followed. He'd be stupid not to.

"And," David continued, "back at the ranch, I secretly met with TL nearly every night to give him a rundown on our day's activities."

I didn't have a response to that one either. I didn't feel double crossed, really. Naive better explained my thoughts. It was naive of me to think I could do such a complex job without TL closely monitoring me.

"Don't take it personally. To my knowledge, he's never just handed over the reins to someone. He *is* in charge. Even when someone goes on a solo mission, like I did to Iowa, he's still on top of it all. That's his job. And that'll be his job until he one day steps down and turns his duties over to someone else."

"Over to you."

"Maybe. Being a strategist is not easy."

"Tell me about it." Suddenly, I missed David so badly I could barely stand it. "I really miss you."

"I miss you, too."

And then the line clicked off.

Later that night I lay wide-eyed, staring at the dark ceiling of my hotel room. One A.M. I knew it was one A.M. because I'd been incessantly checking my watch since my return from the beach.

The air conditioner kicked on. Its rush of air and motored hum muted Jessy's (or maybe Lessy's) soft snore. Beside me, Beaker twitched in her sleep and then rolled to her side.

A hotel exterior light filtered through the curtains' crack, flickering shadows across the walls.

My mind was racing. I couldn't stop thinking about everything that had happened since we got here. I'd started thinking about other stuff in order to get my mind off David and why the line clicked off.

I knew *my* cell phone hadn't cut off. I'd had a full battery *and* all my bars. Believe me, I immediately checked as soon as we got disconnected.

So that meant *his* phone went dead. But did it go dead because of his battery or his bars?

Couldn't be his battery. David always had a charged battery.

Which left bars. That didn't make sense, though. Anywhere

we went we had full bars. Even underground. It was one of the benefits of being members of a high-tech, secret organization.

Two-thirteen A.M.

He wouldn't have hung up on me, would he? Right after telling me he missed me? Was the "miss you" part getting too deep?

Gggrrr. Shut up, GiGi. You're driving yourself insane.

I squeezed my eyes shut and concentrated on not talking to myself. I needed to sleep. Think code. That always relaxed me.

<!Element (%styfon;~%phse;)- -(%line:)>

<Cite<hatru>/Q land="en"-us>

<=*ptth*= /!attstli!/ %csorrtetat%>

Three twenty-one A.M.

Why didn't he call me back? I'd tried calling him back and had gotten his voice mail. In fact—I lifted my cell phone from my stomach and checked the display—no missed calls. No voice mails. No nothing. Nada. Finito. And if I had Parrot's linguistic skills, I'd give it in sixteen other languages, too.

Four forty-two A.M.

Surely lying on my back this long would give me bed sores. Or a flat butt.

Rolling onto my side, I stared at the back of Beaker's head . . .

▦ ▦ ▦

"goood morning, barracuda key, florida!"

I shot straight up in bed.

"It's six A.M. on this beee-u-ti-ful day!"

One of the twins slammed her hand over the alarm radio. "Shut up."

Six A.M.? I must have fallen asleep and gotten exactly—I quickly calculated—one hour and eighteen minutes of sleep.

With a groan, I dropped my head into my hands. This day hadn't started and it *already* sucked.

One of the twins opened the curtains, allowing the morning sun to pour in. Squinting, I held my hands up to block the glare shooting straight into my skull.

Beaker stretched. "What are you, a vampire?"

No, but I felt like one.

Beaker swung her legs over the side of the bed. "You look like somebody broke you into pieces and didn't quite get the puzzle when they put you back together."

With another groan, I fell back into bed and crammed the pillow over my head.

"Good morning, good morning, good morning, how are you? I'm fine, I'm fine, I hope you are, too. Good morning, good morn . . ." I didn't know which twin was singing (and dancing by the way her voice bounced around the room), but I wanted to duct-tape her little mouth and shove her from the room.

One bathroom and four girls did not make good odds, but an hour later, we all managed to be ready. I'd always been a low-maintenance girl. It didn't take much to get me going. Fifteen minutes tops—showered, ribbons tied, and all. Watching the twins made me thankful of that.

I didn't know so much could be done to fingers and toes,

eyebrows and hair, makeup and shaving, and whatever else in preparation for one single day. Heck, it took them fifteen minutes just to apply lotion. It wore me out watching them.

Then again, I was *already* worn out, so maybe that was my problem.

We left our room and joined the other color-coordinated girls trickling through the halls and down the elevator.

TL caught up with us in the lobby and motioned us to follow. He led us down a hall, around a corner, and into a vacant conference room.

That was the good thing about hotels. Lots of nooks and crannies to duck into.

TL pulled the tiny blue pyramid from his pocket and rotated the top. "Eduardo and his men were in their room all night. Parrot translated the Portuguese you recorded."

Portuguese? I'd thought it was Spanish. Guess that's why I wasn't the linguist of the group.

"Everything's definitely on," TL continued. "But they didn't talk times, dates, or locations."

Beaker held her finger up. "So basically we still have nothing."

"No," TL corrected. "We have the recording, pictures, the DNA dust. Some proof. It's a start. We need a location, though, where it's all going down. We need the smuggled chemicals. We need the location of where his buyers will be making the bombs. We need to know how he's shipping them back out. We need Eduardo Villanueva in the middle of it all. And we need to get a tracker on him so we know when he's on the move."

"The simulated mosquito sting," I suggested, "is going to be our best bet. That way we can plant the tracker from a distance."

TL nodded. "I agree. And I want a camera in his room today. No audio function on it, though. We don't want him to pick up our signal if he happens to scan his room for bugs. The IPNC has given us a lip reader." TL handed me a piece of paper. "This is his IP address. Make sure all film goes directly to his computer so he can analyze it and tell us what Eduardo and his men are saying."

I pocketed the paper. Great idea sending silent film to a lip reader. Why hadn't David and I thought of that while we were planning things?

"That's it for me. You two got anything?"

We shook our heads.

TL extended his hand. "Give me one of the simulated mosquito stings."

I slipped my backpack off my shoulder, unzipped the front pocket, and gave him what looked like a mechanical pencil. The stings were cool little devices, able to shoot up to twenty feet. They were a combination of Chapling's technology, my proto laser tracker invention that I'd brought with me from Iowa, and Wirenut's putty-blowing bamboo that he'd used on the Rissala mission. I'd thought Wirenut's homemade device was so neat that Chapling and I had immediately started tinkering with it after Rissala.

Once programmed, the simulated stings worked like those

military missiles that swerve through the air until they find their target. The pencil's lead end held the tracking component, and the eraser served as the release lever. Line the lead up with the target (person), and press the eraser. A tiny chunk of lead would shoot through the air and straight into the person's body, feeling like a mosquito sting.

TL slipped the pencil in his T-shirt pocket. He rotated the pyramid counterclockwise to the off position. "You two go and eat breakfast. No skipping." With that, he strode from the room.

Beaker and I slowly made our way down the hallway back to the lobby.

"How'd your call with David go?"

"Fine. We got cut off." I didn't tell her I'd stayed up all night obsessing over it.

"Huh. That's weird."

"Tell me about it." I stopped at a water fountain and took a quick sip.

"I, uh . . . I saw CJ again last night after I left you at the pool area, as I was heading back to the room."

"You did?" I smiled. "How'd it go?"

Shrugging, she glanced away. "It went all right."

Her nonchalant tone did not match her shy avoidance.

I dropped the CJ subject. Something told me she wouldn't give me more even if I pressed. And pressing, I figured, might ruin our newfound bond.

Crossing the lobby, we entered the meal room. Like yesterday, everyone had already served themselves and been seated.

And like yesterday, Beaker and I loaded up our plates: eggs, strawberries, muffins, bacon. *And* like yesterday, our hearty appetites drew snide attention.

After breakfast, we headed across the lobby into the practice hall. As we walked in, music throbbed from speakers positioned around the room. Contestants were already spread out, stretching, getting ready for rehearsal.

In hindsight I should've had a muffin and called it quits, because here I stood thirty minutes later feeling a bit queasy. Girls surrounded me on all sides, sweating, dancing, ponytails sagging.

With clipboards in hand, the current America's Cheer team meandered through us, stopping here and there, observing, checking things off.

Beaker stood diagonal to me, her jaw convulsively flexing. She needed gum. I'd keep an eye on her in case she blew one of her chemically talented gaskets.

Wearing a head mike, the team leader stood on a riser at the front of the room demonstrating the moves. "Five, six, seven, eight."

She spun, dipped, kicked, swirled, and did about a dozen more fancy things. All around me girls effectively followed her. I barely made it to the kick part.

An America's Cheer member wandered by, stopping a few feet from me. She watched me, her brows slightly puckered. Then she flipped a few papers on her clipboard and checked things off. I could only imagine:

Ana. Red-and-white team. Complete reject. Check.

The clipboard Nazi moved on, and all around me girls snickered.

I rolled my eyes. What losers. Get a life.

"Five, six, seven, eight." Team leader busted into a rapid-fire series of moves.

Yeah, right. Like that's going to happen.

All around me, girls gyrated. I didn't even try.

Wiping my hand across my forehead, I gazed longingly over everyone's heads to the mats stacked along the side wall. I'd give my last segment of code to flop across them for a few seconds.

"Take five," Team leader echoed through the speakers.

Oh, thank God.

I found the closest America's Cheer member and pulled her aside. "I'm going to need more than five. I'm not feeling well. I need to go to my room."

"That's going to cost you points on the competition."

So. "I know." I gave her my best disappointed look. "But I'm really not feeling well."

"All right." She made a note on her clipboard. "Take as long as you need."

"Thanks." For good measure, I put my hand over my mouth and puffed out my cheeks.

She jerked back. "Go!"

Nothing like the threat of impending vomit to make things real. I snatched my backpack from the pile of everyone else's purses and bags, gave Beaker an I'm-out-of-here look, and then bolted upstairs to our room. Finally, some time to work.

I walked into the room and turned on Lessy's and Jessy's signals on my cell phone. Two red dots popped up on my screen. Cranking up my laptop, I keyed in the access code to the satellite. I plugged in the coordinates to our hotel, X-rayed through the roof, and brought up a picture of Eduardo Villanueva's suite.

He and his men sat around the room as if they were having a pleasant afternoon. One read the paper. Another talked on the phone. Eduardo played chess with the last.

Too bad the lip reader couldn't watch them via satellite. It would make things a lot easier than planting a camera. But with cloud coverage and storms between here and Denmark (where the lip reader lived), the image would constantly flicker and go out.

Speaking of which. I froze the image to stabilize it and studied the room's layout. The wide angle camera would definitely have to be placed high in order to film the entire room and all the men.

I zeroed in on the ceiling fan and the globe light attached to it. If I could get the camera inside that globe, it would be the perfect location.

My heart jolted with excitement as a plan clicked into place.

I accessed the secret panel beneath the bed and found The Fly—a nifty little gadget Wirenut had developed way back before he even became a Specialist. It was a wide-angle camera that looked, big surprise, like a fly. Once programmed it would buzz to its destination, land, and begin filming. According to Wirenut, it had enough battery life to last a year.

Sticking my pencil under its tiny wing, I pressed the on button. It fluttered, and I smiled. Cute little thing.

I brought up the software that I had developed for The Fly and, through a wireless connection, programmed it to its final destination—the globe light.

I deactivated The Fly's audio function and then input the lip reader's IP address so all film would be copied to his hard drive.

In mere minutes, we would know what was being discussed in that room.

Climbing on top of the bed, I lifted The Fly to the vent and let it go.

From studying the hotel's blueprints, I knew the ventilation system from my floor connected to the presidential suite. One way or another, The Fly would find its way there.

Reactivating the live satellite, I kept my gaze glued to the ceiling vent in Eduardo Villanueva's living room. Minutes later, The Fly zoomed out, buzzed across the ceiling, and flew straight into the light fixture. None of the men even looked up.

I flipped from satellite to The Fly's software. Sure enough, it had already begun filming.

I wanted to hug both Wirenut and his bug for their awesomeness.

In the bottom corner of my screen a message popped up from the lip reader, acknowledging the transmission.

Good. Almost everything in place.

We had implemented DNA dust, and pictures of it along with swabs would give us documented proof of where Eduardo had been. The Fly provided film of them in their suite. And now I just had to get a tracking device on them longer than thirty minutes to electronically monitor where they were going.

One way or another, we'd know where everything was going down.

▓ ▓ ▓

ON OUR MORNING BREAK THE next day, David texted me. HEY. BEEN BUSY. A LOT OF UNEXPECTED THINGS ARE GOING ON. TELL YOU LATER. WANTED YOU TO KNOW I GOT YOUR MESSAGE.

What unexpected things? BE SAFE, I texted back.

"Ana?" TL approached me in the lobby.

I showed him David's text. "What's going on?" I whispered.

TL shook his head. "I'm not at liberty to say right now."

I *hated* when TL did that.

"Patience," he said.

Patience was usually a strong point for me, but not when it came to all this top-secret stuff. I didn't like not being in the know.

"The lip reader just texted me that Eduardo has a video conference call scheduled in five minutes." He started walking to the elevator. "Let's go. You're going to hack into it. Chapling already knows and has Parrot ready."

My heart gave one giant leap. A video call was exactly what we needed. Hopefully, we'd find out something worthwhile.

TL keyed a message into his cell. "I'll let Beaker know to cover for us."

We rode the elevator up and hurried into my room. I snatched the laptop from my case, powered up, and keyed in my scrambler code. In the bottom-left corner of the screen I brought up The Fly's software and watched as Eduardo opened his laptop. He plugged in an interpreter box and typed in a password. I watched closely, memorizing it.

I zoomed in on the interpreter box and read its model number. Then I zoomed in on the screen and saw which conferencing software he was using.

Chapling appeared in the bottom-right corner in a video feed. "What do you got?"

"He's using the micro parley software," I told Chapling.

"One second." Chapling's fingers raced over his keyboard. "Sending it to you now."

My screen flicked as my laptop accepted the software Chapling sent me.

"Got it," I told him, activating it.

Through the micro parley software, I hacked into the interpreter box on Eduardo's computer and entered his password. The upper-left corner of my screen mirrored Eduardo's computer exactly.

I signaled TL, and he sat down beside me on the bed.

Parrot appeared in the upper-right corner of my screen, wearing a headset.

I ran a quick stereophonic code patching Eduardo's audio

to Parrot. At that exact second, a dark-haired man appeared on Eduardo's screen. He began speaking in another language. Parrot gave a nod to let us know the transmission was coming through.

Chapling's fingers raced across his keyboard again. "That's Eduardo's brother, Pedro."

Parrot began translating simultaneously with the movement of their mouths. He preceded each translation with the name of the person speaking.

"Pedro: Eduardo, how are you?"

"Eduardo: Fine brother, you?"

"Pedro: Fine. I'm missing my son's soccer game."

"Eduardo: I'm missing lunch."

I looked over at TL. "Is this for real? They're talking about stupid stuff."

He shook his head. "Could be code for something."

"Pedro: I ordered pizza for lunch and it came wrong. I had to send it back."

"Eduardo: Did you get your money back?"

"Pedro: No. They made me a new one for a discounted price."

"Eduardo: When's the new pizza getting delivered?"

"Pedro: At the time we previously discussed."

"Eduardo: Are you waiting on me then?"

"Pedro: Yes, I know you'll be hungry."

"Eduardo: And where is it being delivered?"

"Pedro: The emporium."

Eduardo nodded and signed off.

Parrot took off his headset with a shrug. "Sorry, guys."

With a disappointed smile, I waved at him. "Thanks, Parrot."

I clicked a few keys, and he disappeared from my screen.

Chapling lifted his bushy brows. "Obviously the pizza is the shipment."

Oh, I hadn't thought about that. Made sense, though.

TL nodded. "I agree. Get cranking on emporium," he told Chapling, "and see what you can come up with."

Chapling nodded and clicked off.

I powered down. "Now what?"

"Back to cheerleading rehearsal."

I trudged through the hotel beside TL, wishing that call would have gone better. I didn't feel like we'd gotten anything.

For the rest of the day, Beaker and I went about our rehears-al/dance/smiley annoying daily routine. Eduardo and his men didn't move from their suite. According to a text I received from Nalani, they'd even canceled maid service.

Same held true for the next day, too. I didn't want to say anything, but four guys in a room without maid service? Can anyone say yuck?

They did have food service. But the waiter had been instruct-ed to leave the cart outside the presidential suite in the morning and pick it up at nine P.M.

I spent that night restless, thinking about David. I didn't try calling or texting him back. Something was going on, and he didn't need me crowding him. I wanted to ask TL again, but I knew it'd get me nowhere.

At this point, I felt that the mission had stalled. And I was beginning to wonder if it would even come to fruition.

I checked The Fly's film. The lip reader's report came back with nothing significant. Chapling had figured out emporium meant warehouse, but there were dozens of warehouses on Barracuda Key and the surrounding islands. So basically, we still had nothing.

I had morphed into Beaker, snarling at everything and everybody. If Eduardo didn't do something soon, this mission would be over. All my research and planning would go down the proverbial drain.

13

LATE THE NEXT MORNING. the last day of America's Cheer, I stood in the lobby with Beaker, Lessy, and Jessy, tuning out the twins as they prattled on and on about who had said what to whom. In just a few minutes we would go into our final America's Cheer meeting and find out who had made the national team. Our mission cover would be done—we'd have to leave and Eduardo would escape capture once again.

Suddenly, my cell phone vibrated in my pocket, and my whole body jolted. I yanked it free, checked the display, and my heart kicked into overdrive with what I read.

Beaker yanked her phone from her pocket, too.

Simultaneously, we punched in our passwords to decode the encryption, and I read the text message from TL: EV ON THE MOVE. HEADING TOWARD FRONT DOORS OF HOTEL. ETA: 3 MINUTES.

Both our phones vibrated again.

Nalani this time. EV GO.

Our phones vibrated again.

The lip reader. EV MOVING

Jessy and Lessy leaned in. "Lord, someone wants you two pretty bad."

Quickly, I pocketed my phone. "Just our coach."

"Yeah," Beaker agreed. "He can be a real pest."

I gave Lessy a little nudge toward the rehearsal hall. "You two go on in. We'll be there in a few minutes. Remember, today's the last day. We'll all find out if we're part of the new America's Cheer team."

"Yay," Jessy sarcastically enthused, linking arms with her sister. "Don't be late, you two. I don't feel like listening to you get yelled at."

"Or watching you run laps around the room." Lessy hopped in place. "L-A-T-E! Sorry we're late!"

Laughing, Beaker and I waved them on. They disappeared inside the room, and we bolted out the hotel's doors and across the portico to the palm trees lining the other side.

A bellman approached us. "Anything I can help you with, ladies?"

Beaker flashed him a smile. "No thanks. We're fine. We're just, um, waiting for someone."

The bellman bowed. "As you wish."

He backed away, and I slipped my backpack from my shoulder. I unzipped the front pocket and rifled around. Chapstick, pen, lollipop . . .where the heck were the simulated mosquito sting pencils?

Bouncing her leg, Beaker watched me. "Hurry," she murmured.

I stifled the urge *to* hurry. Jerky, quick movements would draw too much attention. This was supposed to be a casual conversation between Beaker and me as we stood here under the palms.

"I'm about to rip that from your hands," she gritted. "Eduardo's going to walk out those doors any second."

Purposefully ignoring her, I continued searching with a tiny bit of panic settling in. They were in here last night. I lifted a piece of paper and underneath lay two sting pencils. My heart gave a relieved beat. Oh, thank God.

I grabbed them and handed one to her. "Remember," I said through a smile, "we're supposed to be hanging out talking. Not about to shoot someone with one of these."

She plucked the pencil from my hand, narrowing her eyes, and I knew she was about to do something ornery. "Oh!" Loudly, she faked a laugh. "Is that what we're supposed to be doing?" Hahahahaha. "Oh, silly me. And to think, one would wonder." Hahahahaha.

Bellmen began to turn and look.

I kept my smile in place as I put my backpack on the ground. "You can shut up now."

"Ohhh," she breathed, dramatically wiping her eyes.

I narrowed mine. Smart a—

The hotel doors opened, and we immediately snapped into our planned positions.

I lifted the eraser end of the mechanical pencil to my mouth and pretended to chew on it. Beaker stepped slightly in front of me to give the appearance I was looking at her instead of over her shoulder.

"So, anyway," Beaker struck up a nonsense conversation, "I

told the guy no way. I mean, what was he thinking asking me that? And then that girl . . ."

Pretending to hang on her every word, I watched Eduardo and his men stride through the hotel's doors. They were all dressed in suits, leaving only their hands, necks, and faces exposed. The only place I could shoot the tracker.

". . . and I was like, no way." Beaker flipped her hand in the air. "I mean, who was she kidding, right? Saying all that. Oh, and then . . ."

Closing my right eye, I sighted down the length of the pencil. One of Eduardo's men stood in front of him. *Good thing I'm farsighted.* The needless thought popped into my brain as I lined up the lead end of the pencil with the man's forehead. With my tongue, I pressed the eraser. A tiny, nearly microscopic tracker sailed from the pencil twenty feet across the portico.

A couple seconds later, Eduardo's man brushed his forehead and glanced into the air. *One down, three to go.*

". . . Mr. Scallione. You remember him? He totally made a pass at me. Did I ever tell you that?" Beaker shook her head. "I couldn't believe it. I was visiting my grand . . ."

Nodding at Beaker's babbling, I handed her my pencil, she handed me hers, and I resumed my eraser-in-the-mouth position. In my peripheral vision, Beaker recalibrated the pencil I'd just handed her, getting it ready for the next usage. To an onlooker, it appeared as if she was merely twirling it as she continued talking.

". . . all that ended, and she made me eat her famous egg casserole. I don't know what's so famous about it." Beaker gagged. "I almost threw . . ."

I bet this is the most brainless yapping Beaker has done in her whole life. Another needless thought, but it popped into my head as I sighted down the length of the pencil, narrowing in on another one of Eduardo's men. He shook hands with a bellman as they exchanged a key. Lining up the lead end of the pencil with the man's hand, I pressed the eraser.

A couple seconds later, he gave his hand a little shake and wiped it on his pants. *Two down; two to go.*

". . . later that night I climbed up on the roof." Beaker propped her hand on her hip. "Guess who was up there? Timmy, our next-door neighbor. Only he didn't look like the Timmy I remember from first gr . . ."

Exchanging pencils with Beaker again, I kept Eduardo and the one remaining man in my sight. Eduardo said something to the man, the man nodded, and then headed back into the hotel. TL was positioned in the lobby. He'd get that one.

". . . the horse's name was Bunny. Or maybe Sunny." Beaker shook her head. "Either way it was the most beautiful horse I'd ever seen. I can't believe my sister got it for gradu . . ."

Putting the pencil in my mouth, I sighted down the length and lined up the lead end with Eduardo's neck. I put my tongue on the eraser, and a bellman moved right in front of Eduardo.

"Crap," I mumbled around the eraser.

Beaker kept right on talking. ". . . do you know what he's

probably going to get me? A set of encyclopedias or something equally boring and educat . . ."

The bellman shifted away. I resighted Eduardo, lined up the lead end, and clicked the eraser.

A couple seconds later, he smacked his neck and looked straight across the portico at me.

My heart lurched.

As carefully, smoothly, and naturally as I could, I opened my right eye and moved my gaze to the left a fraction. I kept chewing on the eraser, pretending to be enthralled with Beaker's prattling, and gave an understanding nod for good measure.

"Keep talking," I murmured. "He's looking right at us."

". . . it's been that way my whole life." Beaker threw her hands in the air. "Anyway. Hey, did I tell you I went to the zoo? It was the saddest thing that poor monkey . . ."

Taking the pencil from my mouth, I gave Beaker all my attention. "The monkey had been abused?" I grabbed her up in a huge hug. "That *is* sad."

She didn't hug me back.

I pulled away, and it occurred to me that I'd never hugged Beaker before. And from her sour face, I gathered she didn't much appreciate it.

Nodding down the driveway, I grabbed my backpack from the ground. "Let's go for a walk." We headed off away from the sun, giving every appearance we were out for a morning stroll.

Eduardo's car passed us about a minute later, and we kept right on strolling until it disappeared from sight.

Beaker and I nonchalantly turned and headed back up the driveway to the hotel. I wanted more than anything to sprint it, grab TL, and book it out of here. But the last thing I needed to do was to draw attention to us.

Reaching inside my pocket, I pulled out my cell phone and clicked over to tracking mode.

Four blue dots popped up—Eduardo and his men. Lessy and Jessy's red dots appeared in the bottom corner of the screen.

Smiling, I put my cell away. "Everything's in place." I turned to Beaker. "You're pretty good at carrying on a one-sided conversation. Mr. Scallione? Egg casserole? Timmy? Bunny? Sunny? Encyclopedias? A monkey?" I laughed. "How'd you come up with all that?"

Beaker shrugged. "I have my moments."

It made me remember all the fake conversations Jonathan and I had struck up on my first mission. I'd gotten such a kick out of saying stuff that took him off guard. It had surprised me more than anyone that I had come up with the things I had.

TL met us in the lobby when we entered. "Twenty-one hundred hours. Be ready." With that he strode off.

Twenty-one hundred hours. Nine o'clock tonight. In under ten hours I'd hopefully see the end to Eduardo Villanueva and finally stop this madman before he ruins another family.

That thought echoed in my mind as Beaker and I quietly opened the rehearsal hall door and slipped inside.

From her spot up front, the America's Cheer team leader pointed across the crowd.

In unison, all heads turned toward us.

"You're late," team leader echoed in her mike. "L-A-T-E! Sorry we're late!" She circled her finger in the air. "Three times around the room and make it look good."

Beaker and I exchanged annoyed looks while snickers filtered across the crowd.

We took off around the perimeter of the room, clapping, chanting, "L-A-T-E! Sorry we're late!"

As when Beaker had chanted her gum mantra, some girls began sarcastically clapping, others bopped in their chairs. I caught sight of the twins on our second time around. They shook their heads in amused pity.

We circled the third time, came to a stop at the front, and went into simultaneous back handsprings. "Go, America's Cheer!"

Everyone leapt to their feet. "Go, America's Cheer!"

Thank *God* this was the last meeting.

▓ ▓ ▓

seven p.m.

We were back in our room with the twins after getting cut from the team. In two hours Beaker and I had to be ready to go, and we still hadn't gotten rid of Jessy and Lessy. And I'd tried, *believe* me. We needed, more than anything, to access the secret headboard panel for supplies.

"You all should go down to the beach for one last stroll," I suggested. "Come tomorrow morning, you'll be heading back to Alabama. No more Barracuda Key, Florida, sand."

Lessy shrugged. "Don't feel like it."

"Come with us." Jessy perked up. "Yeah, let's all go."

Beaker and I exchanged a this-is-not-working glance.

"Nah." Beaker flopped back on our bed. "We don't feel like it either."

Seven thirty-one P.M.

"You two should go into town and gorge on pizza," I suggested. "You know your mom won't let you have any when you get home."

"Come with us." Lessy perked up.

Beaker and I exchanged a glance.

"Nah." Beaker rolled over. "We're not hungry."

Eight oh-four P.M.

"You two should go sit in the hot tub," I suggested. "Make use of the spa facilities before you head back home."

"Come with us." Jessy perked up. "Yeah, let's all go."

Beaker and I exchanged a glance.

"Nah." Beaker shoved a pillow under her head. "I don't feel like getting wet right now."

Eight forty-nine P.M.

I stared at the clock, my jaw getting tighter and tighter. We had to be outside in eleven minutes, and still no luck with the Jessy/Lessy issue. They'd changed into their pajamas and lay under the covers watching TV.

With the way they were settled in, I highly doubted we were getting rid of them.

"You two," I tried one last time, having no idea what to suggest, "should . . . hurry and get dressed and . . . go down to the, um, lounge, and start singing right there. Yeah, that's what you should do." I jabbed my finger in their direction. "If you were *really* serious about this singing thing, you would do it."

Even to my own ears, I sounded stupid.

The twins just looked at me.

I cleared my throat and glanced at Beaker, hoping to get some backup.

She rolled her eyes and fell back on the bed.

I sighed.

A knock sounded on our door. I trudged across the room and opened it.

TL grinned. "Thought I'd take my two favorite girls out for an ice cream to cheer you up for not making the team."

"Wow." This came from one of the twins. "Your coach is so nice. Ours yelled at us for an hour."

Beaker and I grabbed our back packs and followed TL out into the hall.

"Sorry," I whispered. "No supplies."

He shook his head. "Got it covered."

Of course he had it covered. TL had a backup for everything.

In, down, and out the elevator we went. Bypassing the lobby, we cut through a hall and out the back exit door. We jogged past the pool and down the path leading to the beach, followed the moonlit shoreline about a quarter of a mile, then jogged through the dunes and came out at the back side of a grocery store.

A black van sat idling, waiting. TL led us to it and opened the back door. Beaker and I climbed up and sat down. TL followed, shutting the door behind him, and the van pulled away.

I stared across the cargo space at Nalani and a woman sitting beside her. They both wore black jumpsuits and black knit caps.

"Hello, Sissy," the woman greeted Beaker.

Beaker looked up and blinked. "Ms. Gabrier?"

Ms. Gabrier focused on me. "I was Sissy's chemistry teacher back in her old life. I helped her find her way to the Specialists."

"Really?" I smiled. "That's cool."

Ms. Gabrier turned back to Beaker. "I'm here to assist you with defusing the chemicals."

"*You're*," Beaker pointed at her, "assisting *me*?"

Ms. Gabrier inclined her head. "Yes. I've been hearing good things about you."

Beaker furrowed her brow. "You have?"

Amusement played across Ms. Gabrier's lips. "Yes, I have. I always knew there was something special hidden in there."

Beaker stared at her for a few seconds and then glanced down to her lap. Shifting uncomfortably, she cleared her throat.

I looked over at Beaker. She seemed so . . . amazed and honored, maybe even a little humbled.

If Wirenut were here, he'd put her in a headlock and knuckle-rub her. I wasn't a knuckle rubber, so I found a piece of gum in my backpack and handed it to her. She took it and smiled.

TL opened a laptop and turned it toward all of us. A map of Barracuda Key and the surrounding areas filled the screen.

He tapped on an island north of Barracuda Key, zooming in on it. "This is Mango Key. It's connected to Barracuda Key via a bridge."

He tapped again, giving us an aerial view of a warehouse. "This is where Eduardo and his men have been all day. A huge delivery was made earlier today. Mike has confirmed it's chemicals."

"Mike?" I asked.

"Mike Share."

"David's dad? What is he doing here? I thought he was in the protection program." I hadn't seen him since the Ushbanian mission and his rescue. He'd gone into hiding shortly afterward.

TL nodded over his shoulder. "He's driving the van."

My attention snapped to the solid wall separating us from the driver.

"He heard about the operation and put in a special request to come. Remember, he *was* best friends with your father. And aside from that, he has another personal reason for being here. You'll find out soon enough."

Personal reason? If I was going to find out soon enough, why couldn't TL tell me now?

Ignoring my confused expression, TL continued, "Tonight, at twenty-three hundred, Eduardo will commence auctioning off the smuggled chemicals. Buyers, most of whom are known terrorists, have flown in from all over the world. After all the chemicals are sold, they'll begin the bomb-making portion of the evening."

"Sounds like they've put together quite the entertaining night," Ms. Gabrier commented. "How many people are we talking about?"

"Mike has been there all day with surveillance. Eduardo and his men are now up to twenty. There're only thirty-one buyers."

"*Only* thirty-one buyers? That's fifty-one in all." I waved my hand around the van. "We can't take down fifty-one people."

"The IPNC hired us to find Eduardo and track his next moves, which we've done." TL checked his watch. "By now there are close to twenty IPNC agents in place, ready to raid the warehouse. I've brought in Specialists Team One: Piper, Tina, Adam, and Curtis. David met with them earlier and briefed them. They'll be assisting with diffusing the chemical bombs."

Twenty IPNC agents and Team One? Still not very good odds. But then, one highly skilled agent *was* like two or three people. TL, for example, could easily take on three or more regular people and win.

TL looked to Beaker. "How much time will you need?"

"It depends on how far along they are with the bomb. What chemicals they used. How they mixed or premixed the chemicals. There're a lot of factors that will tell me what defuse substances to administer." Beaker shrugged. "Could take me hours."

"As soon as IPNC moves in and the warehouse is cleared, you and Ms. Gabrier get to work. Nalani and GiGi will assist, along with Adam and Curtis." TL indicated a black suitcase next to Ms. Gabrier. "That's got all the supplies you requested. According to intel, the warehouse has been set up like a chem lab. You'll have a lot there to work with. Plenty of supplies."

He ran his gaze over each of us. "This mission has morphed into a size none of us expected. Beaker, stick close to Ms. Gabrier and GiGi to Nalani. Neither of you girls have the experience to be anywhere by yourself."

We nodded, completely agreeing with him. No wonder David had been too busy to text or call me.

Nalani slid a duffel bag from beneath her seat. She pulled out black clothes and handed them to us. "Put these on before we get there."

Beaker and I slipped the loose-fitting jumpsuits over our regular clothes and zipped up. TL did the same. We three put black knit hats over our heads.

TL handed me the laptop. "Cue into satellite. Let's take a look inside the warehouse."

I keyed in the scrambler code, connected to our satellite, and X-rayed through the warehouse's roof.

Sure enough, one half of the warehouse mirrored a chemistry lab with microscopes, tables, safety equipment . . . pretty much exactly what Beaker's lab looked like back at the ranch.

In the other half of the building, boxes and crates filled the center of the room. People dressed in expensive suits stood around, sipping drinks. Men in military fatigues and machine guns lined the walls. Women in skimpy outfits hung on the arms of some of the suited men. Eduardo stood off to the side talking to one of the suited men.

The van pulled to a stop, and the back door immediately opened. A team of gorgeous men stood there all big and muscular, decked out in dark clothes, Kevlar vests, and headsets.

Simultaneously, they all folded their bulging arms and looked into the van.

"Well, well," Ms. Gabrier commented.

I blinked a few times. Yep, definitely real.

14

The gorgeous men helped us down from the van out into a dark, slightly chilly Florida night.

I took a second to survey the new location. Gigantic, grassy sand dunes spotted the landscape, and to my right, the ocean stretched to the horizon. Our van had pulled in between two dunes. Big oak trees bordered the area beyond the sand dunes.

Men and women dressed in matching black/Kevlar/headset outfits milled around. IPNC agents, for sure. A couple of Jeeps and one Humvee sat off in the distance. A satellite occupied the top of a particularly high dune. I saw Piper, Tina, Curtis, and Adam next to one of the Jeeps. Adam caught my eye and gave me a little wave. I waved back.

The whole scene seemed alien. All this high techiness out in the middle of a beach. We should have coolers and lounge chairs and bathing suits. And oddly, I wanted to remind everyone that it was illegal to walk on sand dunes.

"Hey."

I turned around. "David!"

He grinned and grabbed me up in a huge hug.

My heart jigged around in my chest as I squeezed him back. *God*, this felt good.

David let me go and took a step back. "How are you doing?"

"Fine. I just want to get this mission done already."

"I know." David turned a little. "You remember my dad."

Behind David stood Mike Share. He smiled.

"Of course I remember your dad!" I gave him a hug. "How are you, Mr. Share?"

"Fine. Doing great, actually." He pressed a kiss to my cheek. "And how are you, GiGi?"

"I'm good." I pulled away. "TL told me you were driving the van. I couldn't wait to see you. He said you're here for a personal reason." I waved that off. "But I know, it's none of my business."

He chuckled. "You'll know soon enough."

That's what TL had said.

Mr. Share glanced beyond me to Beaker and held out his hand. "I'm Mike, David's dad."

She smiled a little and shook his hand. "I know. I remember seeing you at the ranch after the Ushbanian mission. You can call me Beaker."

I moved closer to David. "Where's the warehouse? And what about the other agents? I see only a half dozen or so here."

"Warehouse," David answered, "is through the woods a half mile west of here. The other agents are already in place."

"Let's move out," TL shouted.

I grabbed my laptop from the back of the van, and Beaker got her small suitcase of supplies. When we turned around, all the IPNC agents had gone. Including Mr. Share and Team One.

Sheesh, they're quick.

TL and David took off at a medium-paced jog, and we followed in pairs—Ms. Gabrier and Beaker first—as Nalani and I brought up the rear.

TL and David led us across the beach, between two dunes, and into the trees. Spooky thoughts popped into my mind as I took things in. Like something out of a fairy tale gone bad.

Hundreds of live oaks towered around us, their knotted arms twisted together like gnarly, long, arthritic fingers. Their branches climbed out and up in a maze of thick coverage. Intermittent moonlight filtered through, casting weird shadows.

I kept my focus on the terrain as we jogged through the dense woods, ducking low branches and hopping downed limbs. These were woods I *definitely* wouldn't want to be alone in.

Minutes later we trotted to the top of another dune. Down a sandy hill about one hundred feet away stood the warehouse. Crouching in the dark tree line, we surveyed the back of it. Fancy cars in neat little rows lined the sides of the place.

A dirt road led out from the front, trailing away through dunes into the darkness. Four exterior lights, one on each corner, glowed softly, providing the only illumination. Night blanketed the rest of the isolated beachy area.

This warehouse was so out of place. Like Eduardo had plunked it down in the middle of nowhere. But then, I knew from the aerial view that TL had shown us that this island north of Barracuda Key sat basically deserted.

Men in military fatigues with machine guns patrolled the exterior. I counted ten in all, which meant ten more guarded the inside. Seemed like a lot. But then we were talking millions and *millions* of dollars here. Eduardo wanted to make sure his investment remained safe.

"I trained a couple of those men," Ms. Gabrier barely whispered. "Years and years ago. Don't underestimate them. They know what they're doing."

"Some of those guys used to be on our side?" I couldn't believe it.

She nodded gravely. "Bad pays better."

I didn't care. It didn't matter how much money someone paid me. I'd *never* turn bad.

TL signaled for me to turn on my laptop.

Stepping behind a tree, I activated the dimmer mode, assuring there'd be minimal glow. I cued into satellite and X-rayed through the warehouse's roof.

Boxes of chemicals sat open, some had already been transferred to the chem lab portion of the warehouse.

"Keep an eye on that screen," TL instructed me. "Tell Nalani as soon as they make their first bomb; then we'll have all the evidence we need and can move in." He turned to Beaker. "Don't forget, Adam and Curtis will be on your defuse team. They know to go straight to the lab."

Beaker nodded, and, signaling for us to stay, TL and David took off into the woods.

I felt bad for Nalani having to be my babysitter. I knew she'd probably prefer to be down in the action. "Sorry you have to stay here with me," I mumbled.

Nalani shook her head. "It's not like that." She pointed out different men on the screen. "Those are all known terrorists. We're raking in quite the bundle on this bust."

Taking my eyes off the screen, I studied the side of her face for a few seconds. "I know about you and TL." He would kill me for saying that.

She glanced over at me with a sad smile. "I know."

Why are you two so distant? I wanted to ask. "Is everything okay?" I questioned instead. "I saw you crying . . ."

Nalani switched her attention to my laptop screen, drawing mine as well. More chemicals had been sold and moved to the chem lab. But no bombs yet. As I watched, Eduardo carried a flask of green liquid to a table.

"Our life is . . . unusual. We, um . . ." she hesitated, like she was trying to decide how much to tell me. "We knew each other when we were kids. We spent time in the same foster home."

Nodding to the screen, she put her finger over her lips, signaling no more talking. I focused in on the laptop as the buyers moved into the lab portion of the warehouse.

Eduardo distributed safety gear, and, as the men suited up, he went to the front of the lab. The men began pouring chemicals, mixing, firing up burners. White smoke trailed upward as one guy poured his solution into a small metal container. He connected a wire and a small timer box.

"That's what we needed," Nalani said. She pulled her collar up and whispered into an attached mike, "Move in."

Turning from the laptop, I focused down the hill at the warehouse.

A patrolman silently dropped to the ground.

I blinked. What the . . . ?

One of our guys pulled him under a SUV to hide him. Wow, I didn't even see him there.

On the other side of the warehouse, another patrolman quietly dropped, and an agent slid him behind a huge palmetto.

I scanned the area, searching for more agents, unable to locate them.

One by one patrolmen dropped, and our guys slid them from view. I didn't ask if the bad guys were dead or alive. I didn't want to know. They may have been highly trained, but turning bad apparently had taken away their skills.

With all ten patrolmen disabled, the place sat very still. I saw nothing. I heard nothing. No good guys, no bad guys. Just cars, the warehouse, darkness, and an occasional frog croak.

I'd never actually watched a takedown of this magnitude before. We'd discussed it once in one of our PTs. But seeing it live . . . well, it was just plain impressive. These agents were amazing.

On cue, everything happened at once. Piles of sand lifted and agents crawled from beneath them. Palmetto branches stirred and other agents slinked out. Shadowed figures materialized from the darkness, hidden only by the night. A tree rustled to my right, and I jumped as someone emerged.

I glanced at Beaker. Her wide-eyed expression mirrored my thoughts exactly.

Wow.

Some of the agents wore black, others green, and others tan. A few had palm fronds sticking to their clothes. They all wore hoods to hide their faces.

No wonder I hadn't seen any of them.

Stealthily, they crept through the night, weaving around the parked cars until they surrounded the warehouse. Six agents shinnied up the aluminum sides all the way to the roof. How they shinnied, I couldn't tell. I saw no ropes or wires. It reminded me of the Rissala mission and how Wirenut had effortlessly Spider-manned it up the side of a castle with air-lock suction cups.

In the moonlight, I saw the agents make hand signals to one another, from the ones on the roof to those on the ground. Quick flashes of gloved fingers, brushing their shoulders, their faces. Like the signals TL used with us.

An agent on the roof threw back a hatch at the same time the agents on the ground crashed through the front door and busted down the back. Light poured out as our guys rushed in.

Gunshots popped.

I flinched.

Screams.

More shots.

Shouting.

My heart lurched. Where was David? TL? Mr. Share? Adam and Curtis and the rest of Team One?

Nalani grabbed the back of my jumpsuit. I looked over at her. Her whole face tightened, and she nodded once, silently telling me to hang in there.

Me? What about her? She had to be scared to death for TL.

I moved my gaze back to the warehouse.

A man in a lab coat bolted out the back door. An agent followed, tackling him to the ground. He planted his knee in the man's back and cinched his hands to his ankles.

More gunshots went off.

My whole body tensed. Had David gone in with everyone else? With their hoods and camouflaged outfits, everyone looked the same. What had David been wearing? My mind raced to remember. Black. He'd been dressed in all black.

Screams and more shots sounded.

God, what's going on? I can't stand this.

I covered my ears with my hands and squeezed my eyes shut. I couldn't look anymore. I couldn't listen anymore. My heartbeat thundered in my ears. My breath rasped.

My parents had died this way. Violently. Gunshots exploding. That horrible sound was the last thing they'd ever heard.

Suddenly, the place fell completely and utterly silent.

Slowly, I opened my eyes and slid my hands down my face.

Nalani let go of my jumpsuit. "All clear." She signaled Beaker and Ms. Gabrier. "Let's do it."

Beaker grabbed her small suitcase, we pulled our knit caps over our faces, and we left the trees to jog down the sandy hill. My heart thumped in my chest in slow, deep surges. We were about to defuse bombs.

Disheveled people stumbled from the warehouse, men dressed in safety gear and the slinky dressed women, all with their hands secured behind their backs. Blood trickled down their faces, their arms, their legs. Most of the women were crying. The men all looked really pissed off.

Agents shouted orders at them, pointing, kneeling them in the sand. With all the gunshots, I could only imagine what the scene was inside the warehouse.

I followed Beaker and Ms. Gabrier through the back door and caught a quick glimpse of blood and bodies. Someone moaned. My gaze flicked to the person making the painful sound. Dressed in a dark suit, a man gripped his bloody stomach as he sluggishly rolled over. Somewhat hypnotized, I watched him, my mind whirling back years ago to the plane crash. To the bodies that had floated past me . . . My vision blurred as I turned a slow circle, trying to recall what I was supposed to be doing.

Nalani steered me toward the chem lab. "Don't look. Focus on the objective."

I blinked my eyes a few times and swallowed, refocusing.

We wound through stacked wooden crates and pushed through

heavy hanging plastic into the lab where Adam and Curtis were already waiting.

"Nobody touch anything," Beaker ordered.

Quickly, yet with the most intense focus I'd ever seen, she began walking around studying the flasks of liquids, bowls of powders, piles of clay, copper wire, magnets, tubes of thick substances, boiling flasks, dishes of crystals. In her chemistry notebook, she jotted down the measurements off scales, weird-looking meters, timers, scopes, syringes, burners, bottles.

Ms. Gabrier gave each of us a heavy lab coat, goggles, and the scenario papers Beaker had drawn up. I swallowed a gurgle of hysteria as I realized a lab coat and goggles would do nothing to protect from a bomb exploding.

Hurry! I wanted to yell at Beaker, but I knew the necessity of intense concentration when everything was on the line. I slipped my black hood off and donned the safety gear.

Beaker cycled back around the room. She pointed to two silver canisters with blue liquid flowing in a glass tube between them. "Curtis. Scenario two hundred and three. You have five minutes."

I blinked. She'd memorized the scenarios? All four hundred and eleven? Oh my God.

Curtis hurried over, flipping through his pages, locating his scenario. Quickly, he silently read it. "What's leum acid?"

"It's that black liquid in the syringe," she answered without glancing up. "It's next to the silver canister."

With a nod he slipped on gloves and carefully took the syringe. I focused back on Beaker.

"Nalani, this one's yours." Beaker indicated a bowl filled with what looked like grape Jell-O. A small copper wire very simply, almost innocently, stuck out the top. "Scenario sixty-eight. Do *not* touch the bowl."

Locating her scenario, Nalani crossed the room. I watched as she picked up tongs, and then I refocused on Beaker. Pick me next, I silently implored. I wanted to get this over with.

Beaker stopped at a flask of boiling pink liquid with yellow smoke puffing up. She inserted a skinny piece of pink paper, brought it out, and studied the end. It turned white. "Adam. Scenario one hundred and twenty-seven."

She moved on as Adam made his way around the table Nalani stood at, reading his scenario as he walked. He stopped, scanned the lab, then went across to where Curtis worked and slid an unused thermometer from the table.

Nervously, I focused in on Curtis and watched as he gingerly unscrewed one of the silver canisters. I glanced back to Beaker. Pick me next, I silently pleaded. My stress was about to explode my brain cells.

She indicated a station with a two-foot-tall silver pot. "Ms. Gabrier. This'll detonate in exactly two minutes."

Two minutes?!

"Scenario four hundred and one," Beaker calmly instructed.

How could she be so calm? And for that matter, how could everybody else? I scanned the room taking in my team's focused, patient movements. I didn't understand. My heart was about to leap from my chest.

"GiGi."

I snapped my attention to Beaker.

She stuck her finger in a gold powder and touched it to her tongue. She waited for a few seconds with her tongue out, the spit on the floor. "Scenario five."

I raced over, my eyes dropping to scenario five. It read vinyl alcohol, odatedrogen, and silver nitrate. Silver nitrate was the only name I recognized. It said to grate metal naph across the top and then stir slowly counterclockwise for ten seconds. My heart gave a relieved beat. Sounded simple enough. Wait a minute, grate? How much. A light scattering or a thick covering? "It doesn't say how much to grate."

"Sprinkle it," Beaker answered. "Like it's salt."

I glanced around my area and located a plastic-wrapped block of what looked like green cheese. Its label read METAL LAPH. Carefully, I peeled the plastic off the green block. A grater sat right beside the bowl of gold powder. I picked up the grater and ran the green block across it, watching as it sprinkled the top. I studied the sprinkles, realizing I salted things lightly. Beaker might salt things heavily. I was dying to ask if she would come look, but went on instinct instead.

Taking a stirring rod, I slowly stirred counterclockwise, watching ten seconds tick by on my watch. What if I stirred slower than her? Or what if she stirred slower than me? I pushed the doubtfulness from my mind and kept going counterclockwise. Ten seconds passed, and I glanced up.

Beaker and Ms. Gabrier stood across the room at a very

intimidating-looking row of fiercely boiling liquids. Ms. Gabrier handed Beaker a blue balloon.

"GiGi," Nalani whispered, dragging my attention behind me. I realized Adam and Curtis were gone and Nalani was already back in her black hood.

She motioned to me. "Let's go. That's the last one. Beaker and Ms. Gabrier will take care of it."

I shuffled over to the side door where she was waiting and took off my safety gear. Slipping my black hood back on, I stepped out into the night and took a deep breath. We headed left toward where all the people still knelt. I checked my watch. Only eight minutes had gone by since I'd disappeared into the lab. Seemed a lot longer.

I surveyed all of our guys, looking for David. But with their hoods and camouflaged outfits, they all seemed alike. One, two, three, four, five . . . I couldn't remember how many TL said we had. Or if he'd even said how many were dressed in black like David. For all I knew, he could've changed into another outfit. I looked at their bodies, unable to distinguish one from the other.

More handcuffed people ushered from the warehouse with our guys behind them.

One of the bad guys strutted out, his head up, all haughty, like he hadn't just been busted. "My father is a very powerful man," he back talked to an agent.

The agent shoved him, and the bad guy went face-first into the sand.

That's the least he deserved.

Nalani and I crossed in front of all the kneeling people. I scanned their angry faces, searching for Eduardo's. I passed by a sobbing woman.

"Shut up," the old man beside her snapped.

These were some of the richest, most powerful people and terrorists in the world. They'd probably never been busted for anything. Most likely they'd always succeeded at getting away with their illegal dealings. They probably thought their money would buy them out of this one.

Sad truth was, for some, it might.

And the women. Boy did they pick a bad time to be a rich guy's decoration.

"I don't see Eduardo," I whispered to Nalani.

She shook her head.

Then it hit me. Maybe he was dead. I wouldn't be able to confront him about my parents. I wouldn't get any answers. And as those thoughts slammed into me, he walked straight out the back door.

I froze.

An agent behind him jabbed a gun in his side, pushing him forward. They strode away from me, past all the kneeling people, and into the night.

Wait. Where were they going?

"No." I sprinted across the sand. Nalani made a move for me, and I brushed her off.

The agent and Eduardo cut the corner of the warehouse, disappearing around the side.

"Wait!" I screamed, bolting after them.

"Stop!" Nalani yelled.

I rounded the corner, eating up the distance between Eduardo and me, and grabbed hold of them both. They stopped and turned.

I shoved Eduardo in the chest. "You killed my parents!"

His lips curved into an evil smile. "Did I now?"

Rage rocketed through my body, vibrating out every pore. I reared back and slammed my fist straight into his jaw.

His head moved slightly with the impact. Blood welled in the corner of his mouth. Staring straight into my eyes, he licked it off and spit it in my face.

I yelled and reared my fist back—

"No."

The female agent's command brought me to a halt, and tears immediately poured out of my eyes.

"Why?" I sobbed. "Why did you kill them?"

"Little girl, I don't know who you are, or your parents." Eduardo shrugged. "If they died, they must have deserved it."

His casual brush-off made more angry tears come. For the first time in my life, I wanted to kill someone. "Y-you took away everything. You made that plane go down. You shot my parents in the head. I-I was only six. You ruined my life."

Blankly, he stared at me. "Ah, yes, the plane crash. Your

father was one of my best men. Such a shame to find out he was double-crossing me. Bad things happen to double-crossers. You need to always remember that."

My breath hitched at his admittance to being connected to my father. "What did you do with my mom's body?"

He shrugged again. "Sorry, don't know what you're talking about."

"My mom's body!" I screamed.

Eduardo's brows lifted ever so slightly. "Sure she's dead?"

"Okay, that's enough," the female agent spoke.

I switched my gaze to hers, and through her hood in the moonlight, I stared into her blue eyes. I had the unnerving sensation I'd looked into those eyes before.

15

THE FEMALE AGENT broke eye contact with me and manhandled Eduardo along. In the darkness, I turned and stared as they strode down the side of the warehouse toward the front.

I took a step toward them. *Wait,* I wanted to yell. *Where are you taking him? Who are you? Do I know you?*

Lightly, Nalani grasped my arm. "Let them go."

"Who is that?" I asked, sniffing.

Nalani shook her head.

I watched as the tall, slender agent led Eduardo away from the warehouse and into the parking area. A black SUV's headlights flicked on.

She opened the back door, illuminating the interior. A person dressed the same as her, in all black with a knit hood, sat behind the wheel.

The female agent shoved Eduardo into the back and climbed in after him. She shut the door, sending the interior into darkness again. The SUV pulled out from the parking lot and onto the dirt road and disappeared into the night.

I turned to Nalani. "What's going on? Who were they? Where are they taking him?"

She shook her head again. "It's out of our hands. The IPNC decides what happens now. I promise you, though, he'll pay for his crimes. He'll pay for what he did to your parents." She gave my hand a tug. "Let's go."

I didn't doubt he would pay. I knew he would. "But who was that agent? That one seemed so familiar. Something about her eyes. Do I know her?" I grabbed Nalani's arm, a thought slamming into me. "They didn't find my mom. She could've swum away. Hidden out. Been pursuing Eduardo ever since. She could still be working rogue for the government. She could—"

"GiGi." Nalani squeezed my shoulder. "There's no way Eduardo would have let your mom live. You know that, right?"

A couple of long seconds passed, and, reluctantly, I nodded.

"He was playing with you just now. Don't let him mess with your psyche."

I sniffed again, drying up the last remnants of my tears.

"You're an analytical person. You see things in black and white, and you don't like gray areas. The fact that your mom's body was never found is a gray area." Nalani released my shoulder. "Sometimes in this business you don't always get black and white. That's the hard truth. Not everything gets answered, resolved."

Taking a breath, my brain and emotions hesitantly acknowledged her words.

The sound of an engine cut through the night, and I glanced

over my shoulder to see a semitruck coming down the dirt road. It rolled to a stop in front of the warehouse.

Handcuffed people shuffled passed me, corralled on both sides by agents. They made their way down the side of the warehouse to the front. The agents opened the semi's back doors, pulled a ramp down, and led the captives up.

Minutes later, the agents filed in behind them, shut the doors, and the semi pulled out.

Nalani took her hood off. "All clear."

I did the same. "What about the dead bodies inside?"

"There'll be another crew here shortly to catalogue evidence and clean things up." She nudged me with her elbow. "By the way, nice punch back there."

I curled my fingers in, noticing for the first time a slight throb. "Thanks."

David rounded the side of the warehouse and nearly smacked right into us. "There you are. You okay?"

Nalani kept going around him toward the back of the building.

Closing the distance between us, I wrapped my arms around his back and pressed our bodies together. I buried my face in his neck, and closing my eyes, I inhaled his familiar scent, took in his warmth, and felt his heartbeat.

David laid his cheek on my head and held me snug against him. I could stand here for eternity wrapped in his arms and die a very content person.

"I couldn't find you," I mumbled. "I was so worried."

"Shh." He tightened his hold. "I'm okay."

He slid his hands up my back, and, cupping the sides of my face, he brought my lips to his. Softly, tenderly, he kissed me, and then pulled back. And still cradling my face, we gazed into each other's eyes. Although neither of us said a word, I knew as I held my eyes to his that our relationship deepened a level.

I didn't know what I would do if anything happened to him.

"As soon as we get home, I'm taking you out." His eyes crinkled. "You and me. Alone. Out. Official date. Yes?"

I smiled. "Yes."

He took a little step back. "Did you talk to Eduardo?"

I nodded. "I hit him."

David lifted his brows. "And?"

"He admitted to being connected with my father. Oh, and that agent that took him. Something seemed familiar about her. Do you know who she is?"

He shook his head. "Sorry."

A throat cleared behind us. "Excuse me, David, I need to speak with you."

We turned to see Mr. Share standing with Beaker.

"How'd it go inside?" I asked her.

She quirked a smile. "Got everything defused. No prob."

"That's great."

From behind them, TL waved me over. "GiGi, over here. Let Mike talk with David and Beaker."

Beaker? Why would Mr. Share want private time with Beaker? I glanced at her in silent question.

She shrugged, as clueless as me.

"Excuse me." I strolled past and headed over to TL.

The three of them wandered away into the shadows of the cars. David and Beaker leaned up against a truck while Mr. Share stood in front of them. The darkness hid their expressions, but I watched them anyway.

TL, Nalani, and Ms. Gabrier headed inside the warehouse, leaving me alone, standing in the sand, staring through the night at David, Beaker, and Mr. Share.

And the more I stared, the more I realized how rude it was *to* stare. So I sat in the sand and made myself look anywhere *but* in their direction.

What the heck was going on?

My mind tried to come up with answers . . . Mr. Share wanted to speak with Beaker about her restoration solution? No, that didn't make sense. He was a computer guy. Why would he care about chemistry? Unless, maybe he wanted to put her solutions in a computer? But then, what did that have to do with David?

No. There was absolutely no reason why Mr. Share would need to talk with David *and* Beaker.

TL emerged from the warehouse. "Let's go."

"What?" I stood. "But what about Nalani and Ms. Gabrier? An-and Beaker, David, and Mr. Share?" We weren't just going to leave them, were we?

TL charged up the hill toward the trees. "Nalani and Gabrier are staying for cleanup. The others will be along shortly."

"But . . ." I followed behind TL. "But I didn't get to say 'bye to Nalani."

TL entered the woods. "You'll see her again."

I glanced over my shoulder. Mr. Share still stood in the darkness with David and Beaker. None of them had moved. The back door to the warehouse sat open, with bright light shining out. Shadows flicked inside as Nalani and Ms. Gabrier moved about.

"GiGi," TL called, "pick up the pace."

I jogged through the woods and caught up. "For the record, I hate secrets. I'm dying to know what's going on with David and Beaker. And for another record, I *never* want to be in charge of a mission again." Way too much stress.

TL chuckled. "Duly noted. At least you tried, but not everyone's a leader."

This mission had definitely taught me that. "I'm sorry for being an idiot and making bad decisions?"

"Everyone makes mistakes. Always remember that."

I wondered how long it would be before I truly earned back his total trust.

"What about that family?" I asked, stepping over a stump. "The one I overheard Eduardo talking about . . ." Killing. I couldn't quite finish the sentence.

TL nodded. "Everything's fine."

He didn't elaborate, but if he said everything was fine, I believed him.

We didn't talk the rest of the way through the woods. A half mile later we came out the other side. Our van still sat there in between two dunes with a Humvee behind it. Everything else was gone. The jeeps. The other Humvees. The satellite.

A red-haired man helped a little red-haired girl climb up into the Humvee. Inside sat another little girl and boy, also redheads, and a grown woman. The man shut the door, climbed behind the wheel, and cranked the engine.

One of the tiny girls watched me through the window as they pulled away. She sent me a sweet little wave and I returned it. "That's the family, isn't it?"

TL came up beside me. "Yes. Dad's a chemist. Eduardo had kidnapped his kids and wife in order to get him to do what he wanted."

I watched them drive safely across the sand. "They're safe now."

"Yes, they are. Thanks to you. If you hadn't overheard Eduardo's conversation, it's likely we would have never found out about them."

TL's words brought me peace. Thanks to me, a whole family would go on living happily together.

Dialing his cell phone, he stepped away. I stowed my laptop inside the van.

Leaning up against the vehicle, I stared at the woods and waited for David and Beaker to appear.

The ocean swished to shore, TL mumbled softly in the background, an occasional gnat flew past.

And still I waited, my gaze fixed on the trees . . .

Some time later, David stepped from the live oaks first, followed by Beaker. I searched both their faces for signs of anything. But neither of them looked at me, or at each other. They kept their focus down as they approached.

I pushed up from the van. "Hey."

"Hey," David mumbled.

Beaker said nothing.

I took her supplies and put them in the vehicle. "Where's Mr. Share?"

David tossed a backpack in behind her supplies. "He's staying behind to help with cleanup."

"Oh."

And then the three of us lapsed into silence with the two of them staring at their shoes.

Mind telling me what's going on? I wanted to ask, but waited patiently instead for one of them to speak.

"Let's go." TL climbed into the driver's side.

We loaded into the back, and TL pulled out.

Beaker sat beside me and David across. I looked from one to the other and back to the first, waiting for someone to say something. But neither spoke as they stared at their laps.

"Oh good God. Someone tell me what's going on." So much for patience.

David glanced across the van at Beaker.

She shrugged a shoulder. "Go ahead."

He scrubbed his hands down his face, and, leaning forward, he propped his elbows on his knees. He sighed, fixing his attention on the van's flooring.

Seconds passed, and I waited, suspended in suspense.

What? I'm dying here, people.

"The government," David began, "contracted my dad to develop a computerized DNA program. It compares and contrasts the different chains of the double helix. It'll be used in criminal investigations and for medical reasons like organ matching for donors."

David cleared his throat, still focusing on the floor. "My dad's been testing the program, loading up all the DNA currently on file. He pulled up all the DNA that matches his. Of course, my name popped up . . . but so did Beaker's."

I glanced between them. "I don't understand."

David swallowed, and the gurgle echoed in the cargo space. "Did you know my grandfather was a gifted chemist?"

"No. Are you trying to tell me you two are distant cousins or something?"

He rubbed the back of his neck. "Do you remember I told you my mom left when I was a little boy?"

"Yes."

"My dad was on assignment in Jacksonville, Florida, undercover as a fisherman when he met this woman. He was really upset and got drunk one night, and . . . long story short, he had no idea she got pregnant."

My heart slowed to a steady, knowing thump. "Are you saying . . . ?"

David brought his eyes up to meet mine. "Beaker and I are half-sister and -brother."

we'd been back at the ranch for a week when I stepped from the ranch house into a brisk, sunny, California day.

Off to the right, Parrot galloped his horse across the pasture, with Bruiser holding on tight behind him. Her excited squeals carried on the wind.

Wirenut and Cat came from the side of the house, hands linked, strolling toward the barn.

Mystic and Adam, from Team One, climbed into Adam's car, waving as they pulled down the driveway. Piper, also from Team One, followed them in her car. I'd overheard them say they were going to pick up their friends and head into town to a basketball game.

I heard David's laughter and glanced left. He and Beaker sat on a bench under a sequoia tree. Beaker had transformed back into Goth. She listened while David animatedly described something. They'd been spending a lot of time together over the past week. In fact, he'd spent more time with Beaker than with me.

I didn't care. I was happy they were happy.

Sitting down on the front step, I studied the two of them. Now that I knew they were brother and sister, their similarities popped out at me: their smiles, the shape of their faces, and oddly enough, their legs.

Beaker favored Mr. Share more than David did. I could only imagine what Beaker must be feeling. Meeting a father she never knew she had. Did it make her feel complete? Finished some-how? Did it answer questions she'd always had? Did the pieces of her life puzzle fit together a little better?

I was happy for her, truly I was. But I envied her a little, too, being reunited with lost family. What I would give for that. *Sure she's dead?* Eduardo's question floated through my mind. No, I wasn't sure my mother was dead. How could I be if her body had never been found? Surely, if TL knew something different, he would've told me by now. But TL may not even know one way or the other about my mother. One thing was for sure, if she was still alive, we'd find our way to each other somehow.

My gaze and thoughts drifted back to Beaker. She'd come a long way since first finding out about the Barracuda Key mission. She'd been tested from all sides, emotionally and physically. And I'd learned a lot about her, too. I understood her better now. Underneath all that gruffness beat a sweet heart. It just took a while to find it. It reminded me that all the members of my new family had come from different places, different situations. Our unique backgrounds helped form each of us into who we are now. Beaker had taught me to look beyond a person's appear-ance to what lay beneath.

Of course, I'd never admit she'd taught me anything.

The door behind me opened. I glanced over my shoulder to see Mr. Share come out. He smiled and touched my head as he stepped around me.

He crossed the yard to the tree David and Beaker sat under. Mr. Share said something, and Beaker nodded. With a slight smile, she stood. He put his arm around her shoulders, and the two of them walked off across the property.

David watched them for a few seconds and then pushed up from the bench and came across the yard toward me.

My stomach flip-flopped as I watched him approach.

He sat down beside me on the step, stretching his legs out in front of him. We sat in companionable silence, our legs barely brushing. After a long minute, he turned and looked at me. I returned his look, curious about what he wanted. But he just continued staring, not saying anything.

I thought back to weeks ago when we'd been in the elevator and he'd done this same deep looking. "What do you see?" I repeated the same question I'd asked him weeks ago.

David's eyes crinkled. I *loved* when they did that. He reached over and trailed his finger along my jaw. "I see beauty that almost makes my heart ache. And not just beauty on the outside." He touched his finger to my heart. "Beauty in here, too."

My heart slammed so hard against my chest wall, I knew he had to feel it, too.

He gave his head a little shake. "When did I become so mushy," he noted with a chuckle.

I smiled at that. I liked him mushy.

Suddenly, I thought of David's first solo mission involving me, before I'd even heard of the Specialists. "How hard was it for you when you came to Iowa to . . ." I didn't want to go into the details. "Well, to get me."

David linked his pinky with mine. "It was hard lying to you.

TL and I had quite a few heated discussions about it when I would report in."

"You did?" And to think I'd spent all that time in Iowa dealing with my crush on David, and he'd been struggling with his first mission because of me. So it was quite possible even back in Iowa he liked me more than he let on. He'd said he'd been fighting the whole like-me-as-a-friend/like-me-more thing for months. How long, exactly, had the battle gone on?

I wanted, no, I *needed* to know when he knew he liked me. Love at first sight? Or something he had to warm up to? Not that he'd mentioned love, but you know what I mean. "David, can I ask you one question, and then I promise I'll never bring it up again."

He waved me on. "Whatcha got?"

"Way back when you first met me, even though you called me your little sister, did you like me but didn't want to admit it? Or did I slowly grow on you?" I hoped he didn't think my questions were stupid.

Playfully, he groaned. "Why do girls always have to know more?"

I waited.

"Yes. Okay? Yes. I thought you were hot when I first met you."

I grinned. "You thought I was hot?"

"And klutzy."

"Hey!" I bumped my shoulder to his, enjoying the fun. "Did you know I liked you back in Iowa?"

David bumped my shoulder back. "How could I not when you fell all over yourself every time I came around."

My jaw dropped. "I did *not*." Actually, I had.

He put his arm around me, and I scooted closer as we lapsed into more silence. Idly, we watched Mr. Share and Beaker stroll across the grass, going farther and farther away.

"How's it going with the get-to-know-you-as-a-sister thing?" I asked.

"Good. Beaker said she met some guy CJ in Barracuda Key." He chuckled. "I've only been her brother for a week, but, weirdly enough, I'm feeling protective."

"What'd she say about CJ?"

"Just that she figured out they really didn't have anything in common."

David's and my phone call from last week popped into my mind, and I finally asked the question that had been bugging me. "Why'd we get disconnected last week? Ya know, when you called?"

"Chapling cut in. That's when I first found out my dad was coming to Barracuda Key."

"Oh." That made sense. And to think I'd obsessed over something so simple.

David leaned over and kissed my neck. "What about that date?" he asked.

"What about it?" I flirted back.

bzzzbzzzbzzz.

With a sigh, I glanced down at my cell clipped to my jeans.

***. TL's stat code.

I looked at David. "I can't believe this."

He pushed to his feet and held his hand out to me. "Here we go again."

I took his hand and let him pull me up. "I can't believe I ever threatened to leave. I don't know what I'd do without this place. Without all of you."

David squeezed my hand. "We, *I* don't know what I'd do without you."

My face warmed at his comment.

He gave my hand a quick squeeze and led me inside the door. "I'm glad you're still here."